Creative Writing Heals
Volume 7

A new collection from Converge writers
at York St John University 2024

Creative Writing Heals: Volume 7
First published in 2024
by Writing Tree Press

All rights reserved. No part of this publication may be reproduced, stored in a database or retrieval system, or transmitted, in any form or by any means, without the prior permission in writing of the publisher, nor be otherwise circulated in any form of binding or cover other than that in which it is published and without a similar condition including this condition being imposed on the subsequent purchaser.

© 2024 respective authors and illustrators
Cover art © 2024 by Stephanie Jardine

The moral rights of the authors have been asserted.
All characters and events in this publication, other than those clearly in the public domain, are fictitious, and any resemblance to any real person, living or dead, is purely coincidental and not intended by the authors. The right of Helen Kenwright to be identified as the editor of this work has been asserted by her in accordance with Section 77 of the Copyright, Designs and Patents Act 1988.

For information contact:
Writing Tree Press, Unit 10773, PO Box 4336
Manchester, M61 0BW
www.writingtree.co.uk

Dedication

This volume is dedicated to Nick Rowe, who retires from York St John University this year after founding Converge in the summer of 2007 and leading us ever since.

Converge would simply not exist without him, and he has wholeheartedly supported *Creative Writing Heals* since its very first volume. His delight in our writers' work has led to its inclusion in conferences, exhibitions and readings in staff meetings. Many visitors to Converge have left with a copy of *Creative Writing Heals* in their hands, ensuring our writers are widely heard.

Thank you, Nick. We all wish you a wonderful retirement, a well-earned rest and lots of time to read!

Contents

FOREWORD 7

WHY I WRITE 9
Cate Wilder

TWO POEMS ON THE THEME OF ADHD 15
Sue T

NARROW ESCAPE 18
Karen Wilson

A MAN ON A HILLTOP 20
K. Delmara

OH NO, NOT AGAIN 25
Chad Copley

THE DANCE 28
Lorna Weaver Dutton

MISS NICELY AND FRIENDS 30
Virginia Sellar-Edmunds

NORTHERN LIGHTS 36
William Davidson

MERMAID 37
Yeti Hammond

CHICKEN BONES..39
Gemma Fawcett

THE MAGICK WAND..42
L.D. Ethrae

FANTASY TUTORIAL: How To Form A Party.... 45
Junior Mark Cryle

HOME..50
Carol Coffey

A COACH DRIVER'S DAY 53
Catherine Pemberton

THE FALL 58
Glenne Shearer

GOING TO THE ZOO 60
Keith Myers

TICK TOCK..62
Christina

THE HOME OF NEW BEGINNINGS 68
Dawn Skelton

THE BALANCING OF TWO SIDES 72
E.J.

DODGY MEAT 73
Michael Fairclough

LOVERS AND YORK 80
John F Goodfellow

RUSTY RAILS 82
Kevin Keld

TRUE CRIME 84
Helen Kenwright

GRANDMA, SMOOTHY CHOPS AND THE CANDLE FIRE
Esther Clare Griffiths……………………………………………..85

THREE POEMS 90
Paul Francisco

THE CHEQUE'S IN THE POST 93
Nic Campbell

THE MORNING LIGHT 95
Enoch Mcfadden

BLOODSTAINED-GLASS 98
Minnie Lansell

TILL DANCE, DO US PART 105
G.V. Terolli

THE TALE OF THE DISAPPEARING COAT 106
Lee King

NEW BOOK 108
Sue Leung

LIGHTNING STAR SCENE 109

James Wilson

THE FINAL GOODBYE 116
Lauran Kay Ransom

THE HOLY TRINITY 118
  S J L

DANCING MICE 122
Sheryl Cunningham

POEMS 126
  Angela Bridge

ACKNOWLEDGEMENTS 129
ABOUT OUR AUTHORS 131
ABOUT CONVERGE 137
ABOUT THE WRITING TREE 139

Foreword

Producing *Creative Writing Heals* is my favourite part of the academic year, as the Converge community shares the fruits of a year's study and practice in Creative Writing. Each year we are impressed again and again with how much our students have achieved.

We don't set a theme for our writers for *Creative Writing Heals*, but it's astonishing how one tends to emerge regardless. What really strikes me in this year's collection is how strongly the voices of our writers appear. Whether the topic is dance, religion, fantasy role-playing games or experiences of mental health, each writer has their own unique and passionate creation.

When asked to suggest some ideas for the blurb for this book, one of our students suggested: 'We speak for those who have hitherto had no voice.' In no Creative Writing Heals volume has this been more true.

Our writers really pour their soul into their work. Writing for publication is an arduous (if loving) task of drafting, reworking, polishing and tweaking, but I think you'll agree with me that all that effort has really paid off. With poetry, flash fiction and short stories here there's something for every occasion, and I hope you enjoy them all.

Helen Kenwright
November 2024

Why I Write
Cate Wilder

A writer writes for a number of eclectic reasons.

These are mine.

I write to communicate. To tell my story, and that of others. I write to shine a light on the past; warts and all. I write to reflect on life's experiences; characters and events merge as narratives are brought to life. Through writing I gain new insight and new insight brings new opportunities. Perhaps even catharsis.

I write to illuminate the present and inform the future; one we may not be ready for. This moment of writing has already become the past. How fleeting that moment is and yet, how important. I write to ease the pain and suffering of life; the anxiety and the stress and equally to share the joyous moments that befall us all. I write because I choose to; because I can.

I write to share my experiences as a woman, an activist and a feminist. I am angered at the impact of misogyny; racism and inequality; violence and hate. I write to share political writing and personal viewpoints. I write to illuminate injustice; to shine a light on the heroines and heroes of our time and those of yesterday. I write because personal narratives need to be told.

I write to expand my language; to evoke a memory of a feeling long since buried. I write to provoke a response. I write to call forth; to summon; to speak my truth. I write to empower, to make sense of life and the world in which we live. I write to connect with who I am. To strengthen my voice. To gain insight. To understand.

We all live life through our unique perspective. I write to leave my imprint. As new memories replace old, I write to preserve them.

Contemporary society offers writers a panoply of opportunities for the socially conscious writer. The internet has expanded our world beyond expectations, beyond the confines of our front doors. Social media likewise. Blogs; journal articles; petitions; poems; prose; letters to the editor; to our MPs, even tweets, all help to raise the voice of the disempowered. Used wisely these catalysts have the potential to shock the world into action; to define the undefinable. It has the power to open up a discourse through which we can all share ideas, values and beliefs. It calls to action those who are voiceless. It makes the silence deafening.

Writing expands the universe. It reaches every nook and cranny. Through social media we bring stories to life; we galvanise society; strengthen a call to action, and in so doing, we create everlasting, unwavering change. But, using social media is not the only way. It is not a panacea. As with violence; it is not the answer. There was no social media in the 1960s when American people stood firm against racism; discrimination; hate and oppression, or when women fought for suffrage in the UK. Nor was there any social media when the Berlin Wall came down and along with it change on an unprecedented scale. But there was a sense of solidarity. There was hope. There was passion. There was a recognition of the need for change. There was a belief that things could be different. There was the motivation. There was the drive.

When I write, all these emotions come to life. I take a stance. I open my heart and my soul. I look at the world through a lens of compassion and understanding. As an academic I write to entwine the views of others with my own. I write to persuade; to influence; to analyse; to inform.

I write to challenge the rhetoric; the oppression; the status quo and the downright ridiculous. I write to make the world a better place.

I want my writing to be all encompassing, creating a strong unadulterated covenant through which we can change the world together. Only when we step inside someone's else's world, when we show compassion; empathy and understanding, can we truly make a difference.

I want my writing to help shape the voice of others. To amplify what they hear and see. To endorse what they feel. I want my writing to help turn passion into positive action. And when it happens, I want a promise that such passion will never become the oppressor. The perpetrator. The judge and jury. The executioner. Instead it will become the protagonist, whose actions stir a sense of hope, benevolence and mutual respect. Let passion change the world; not hinder it.

In years to come, when you are 'pushing up the daisies' how do you want to be remembered? For your voice? Your humanity? Your compassion? Your impact? Your aspirations? Your love for humankind? What? Decide right now who you want to be. Decide your why. Your how. Reach out to others and give them a hand. Through compassion you can do this. Through dialogue, likewise.

Dialogue creates an emotional connection. Hearing personal stories adds strength to a life lived; the torment felt; the suffering witnessed. It illuminates injustice. It opens up an abundance of care. Agony is heard in the tremble; the quiver. It is seen in the tears; through the eyes of despair. It is seen in the empty pockets; in the hungry faces. It is witnessed in the abject misery.

Writing for social change has the power to shift public opinion; question the unquestionable; challenge the unchallengeable. It has the power to influence. Get the right people, in the right place, at the right time and we can move mountains. By clearly articulating the problem, we can work collaboratively to find a solution. It doesn't have to be at national level, local is just fine. It may be all that is necessary.

Become a voice of influence. Challenge the arrogance; the nonsense; the self-importance, of those, who through their actions only feather their own nests; feed their own egos. Write to the council; go to meetings; lobby parliament, lift high the voice of the voiceless. Through action we can create a more just and equitable society. A fairer society where wisdom, compassion and selflessness are the guiding forces; not greed or wealth. Not hate or violence. Don't let power be wielded against you. Find the right message and let your enthusiasm be your powerhouse; your motivating force. We all need to live in a better world. When people take positive action, they become the impetus for positive change.

If you write, encourage others to write with you. It can amplify those forgotten voices. The meek; the mild; the unheard; the disempowered; the forgotten. It can make a difference. It can change the all-pervasive narrative. Put your experience, your love of humanity to good use. Call out the naysayers. After all, chapters in history, that's all we are. Moments in time, that's all we have. It's how we use those moments in time, how we decide the part we want to play, that will undeniably make all the difference.

Writing opens up a door to new possibilities and new ideas. Writing can help develop our unique voice, our self-awareness. It piques our curiosity and our passion. It tells the story of humanity. What makes us human.

Writing for me has become a life strand. I write daily. It helps me to reflect on life. It helps clarify thought; tempers idealism with realism. It helps nurture an inquisitive mind;

to gain insight into the lives and perspectives of others. It galvanises my influence, enables me to build an audience; to become a voice to lead. It makes me a better writer. Sometimes, I write nonsense; sometimes it's a line or two, but through my perseverance it builds and when it builds it takes shape and effortlessly becomes a work of art. Through my writing I have discovered my voice. I have discovered I have a talent. I have a desire to see things as they should be, rather than as they are. And whilst writing stirs a degree of anxiety; of hopelessness; of anger and of sorrow, it also provokes a sense of understanding. It strengthens my knowledge; my enthusiasm to collaborate; to rouse others to action; to change the rhetoric; to imagine the impossible; to make the unbelievable, believable.

Through my writing I have experienced epiphanal moments. I gain insight into why I am still here, and when I share my writing with others it becomes transformed. Writing requires energy. Activism requires energy. Emotion fuels the energy and the energy persuades. Through my writing I embark on a personal story of discovery. I learn to navigate the maelstroms; the peaks and troughs of life. Writing for social change relies on the ego of the writer to believe they can make a difference - or why bother?

Good writing takes courage. It takes guts to have my name out there. Not everyone will like my work. But does it really matter? No-one interprets events quite the way I do. No-one feels what I feel. Experiences life, the way I do. Only I can bring my innermost thoughts to life. Only I can bring them to fruition, creating a profound and inspired existence, through which I experience a world less ordinary.

When I write, I write through a process of deep reflection, at a level which creates a sense of peaceful knowing and profound self-awareness.

Such a deep level of reflection often brings with it catharsis, creating a sense of peaceful knowing and a deep level of self-awareness. It allows my narrative to come to life. It allows me to push my curiosity; to strengthen my courage. It generates a sense of adventure and a willingness to experience what lies beyond.

I'm always looking for the next adventure; the next opportunity, and undeniably they come my way. I never give up; well not easily, and I strive to make the world a better place.

Occasionally, I bring others along for the ride.

Why not join me?

We all need to make a difference. No matter how small. Collective action is the key. But we have to keep going. We need to keep attending the meetings. We need to keep calling out those who care little about the community; concerned only about themselves. But, until caring and empathic people come together, the need for change will be forgotten. The noise will die down. And it will be just another day at the office. Just another day that a child dies needlessly. Just another day that an elderly person dies alone. A mother goes hungry to feed her children. Just another day when a tragic error is made. A woman is murdered by the very person who purports to love her.

But, enough of the rhetoric. I'm asking myself right now - What can I do to make a difference? Please I urge you, ask what can you do?

A quote sits in a frame at the side of my bed - it says, 'Let her sleep for when she wakes she will move mountains.' Each morning when I awake… I intend to do just that.

Two Poems on the Theme of ADHD
Sue T

1. Big Rooms (my first day at Converge)

The thoughts in my mind went all blind,
Floating through lights with bright clean floors,
SOUNDS and SIGHTS of the BIG ROOMS is quiet gloom,
But also it IGNITES my thoughts of delights,
I hear LOUD voices, with one ear alert,
There's a silence about this but still go along,
NEEDING to do this is all i hear,
My thoughts of ACHIEVING,
Of getting it done,
Sitting and listening,
It will be DONE,
The thoughts in my mind
Have just BEGUN.

2. Exploding Snail Brain

I've got Mental Health, and I know it,
It goes everywhere with me,
In fact I do its head in too, going around day after day,
Thinking and thinking, it never stops.
I want it to stop, but it doesn't.

LISTS, LETTERS, MEETINGS,
NEW THINGS, APPOINTMENTS, PEOPLE,
NO, NO, NO, YES, NO,
You have become a snail,
No Brain,
Like a brain breakdown,
Except it keeps going and going,
Chugging chugging,
No one sees, no one hears,
Trying to be normal for yourself,
Dignity, yes.

Under all this MENTAL HEALTH we want respect and understanding,
Like for instance my brain can think of
NOW TOMORROW FUTURE and PAST all in one moment,
You have hiccups, fast pulse,
Brain freeze, become dizzy,

Sweaty, WHAT IS IT BETTY!!??
Clumsy,
Forget the day,
Yes, it is Mental Health, GET IT, GET IT, GOT IT.
One day in my life I found it was me,
           ADHD!!!!

Illustration by Stephanie Jardine.

Narrow Escape
Karen Wilson

I wake up. My head is pounding, and I have no memory of how I got home last night. At least I'm in my own bed. I'm fully clothed, and it feels as though I didn't take my make-up off. I've got one shoe on. I know because I can feel it digging in and my blister is still raw. My foot is hanging out of the bed, on the end of its leg. Thankfully, both are still intact. I look at my phone and sift through the evidence, trying to piece together some of the evening's events:

- A text from Pumpkin Cabs at 11.59pm: 'Your Driver is outside, please look for a White Toyota Prius.'
- A new number added before that at 11.30pm with the message, 'Call me.'
- Several missed calls from that same number, starting at 7am today, then a text at 9am: 'I've got your shoe, you dropped it when you ran off to get in the taxi. Send me your address and I'll drop it round today.'

Oh shit, I remember him now, and I really do not want to see him again. I'm not replying to that, I'm staying in bed. All day if I can get away with it. I check Facebook and see an update in the Town Gossip Group: 'There's a weird bloke going round this morning knocking on doors and offering to marry anyone who fits into some old shoe he reckons to have found after a party last night.'

Jesus Christ. I turn my phone off and get back under the duvet, but not before I get a sick bucket to put beside my bed.

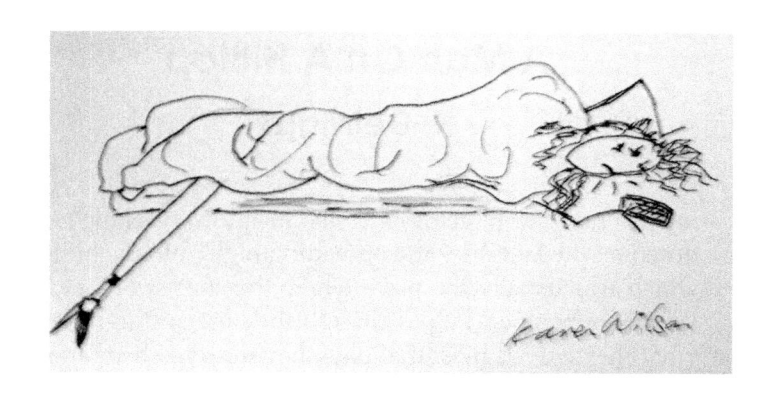

A Man On A Hilltop
K. DelMara

Intense heat swept across the vast meadow, reaching right down by the lakeside, and spreading high onto the hilltop, which was usually the place where the coolest breeze hit. Wildflowers stood tall, as though the heat and light were what they craved most that day; they too stretched far and wide over the meadow, along the lakeside and way up high on that hilltop, where he sat cross-legged, looking down on it all.

Aakil was an elderly man, who had travelled hundreds of miles and countless journeys to be in the place he was now, and it was just as he remembered. He had always loved nature, especially the wildflowers: vibrant red poppies, purple centaurea, yellow buttercups and dandelions surrounded him. His heart swelled at the abundance of colour, the softness of the grass and the clear blue sky above, despite the aches and pains in his frail body, he knew could give way at any moment.

Life was fragile like that.

With closed eyes, he turned his attention inwards, just as his wisest teachers had taught him to do.

Deep raspy inhales followed by long, heavy exhales moved through his body rhythmically, with the occasional coughs and splutters that could not be helped.

He opened his eyes and looked up at the sky, searching for answers.

What does it all mean - what was it all for?

A soft breeze blew around the hilltop and a bee buzzed frantically around him, as he coughed some more.

Back home, a medical doctor had given him two months, after tests that showed a failing heart and a brain tumour;

both had made life difficult, unbearable at times, and the long, drawn-out suffering had been intense. His whole identity had been put into question – and question it he did. The heart and the brain are two of the most vital organs in the human body, and for now, this was the body where his soul still lived. These were the thoughts that plagued him, every minute of every day and way into the night, when all else seemed to be resting.

He sat there completely alone, breathing slowly, noticing the places where it hurt and the places it didn't, noticing the grass beneath his hands and the breeze on the back of his neck, and he felt all of it. Tears trickled down his crinkled cheeks, though he did not try to wipe them away or hold them back like he usually did, after all there was nobody else around him now, nobody to see him or his pain, so what did it matter if he sat on a hilltop and cried.

Sadness settled like a thick fog, heavy and deep, encapsulating his mind to the point it felt it may devour him completely. Loneliness followed like a single slow-moving dust particle that seemed to hold so much power, despite the sense of nothingness and emptiness that it brought... and then came anger that blew in like a gale at full force, so much so that it made him want to hit back, hard... but there was nobody in which to direct that heavy blow, only himself. Aakil sat in stillness with the anger for a while, his hands buried in long grass, until slowly, very slowly, it shifted like a grey cloud that moved across a vast sky, leaving him alone once more with sadness. Though somehow, he felt less lonely now, as he looked down at his hands and then gazed softly at the single red poppy on his right that had been there all along. He kept his gaze upon its black centre and vivid red petals that wrapped themselves around it, until the sadness grew lighter, softer, and more distant.

He must have been sitting on that hilltop in deep

intimacy with those emotions for at least an hour as they moved around inside of him, some taking precedence over others till it was time for them all to leave the gathering.

As the emotions departed and a space was created, new thoughts and questions came into his mind, subtle messages telling him to keep going and to dig a little deeper – though from where they came, he did not know.

Do I exist right now if there is no one here to see me?

Does this failing heart, this brain tumour exist here, where there are no doctors to diagnose them, no hospitals to treat them?

Aakil had noted how whenever he got on a train and travelled away from the source of his problems, they had felt different – he had felt different. This was until he went back of course, and so the question of one's environment and its importance in maintaining good health, often arose in his mind. He thought back to what he had read about plants and when they start to wilt, then it was time to change their environment. This particular environment on the hilltop, surrounded by wildflowers, had always been important to him; it was here where he had his first realisation that there was something much bigger than the mundane existence he had been conditioned to believe. It was here where he had learned to meditate and connect to that something deeper. Aakil had dedicated his life to studying aspects of life such as suffering and healing, finding one's purpose, connection and all the things in between, and so the irony that he was now facing death was not lost on him, though perhaps this was where the questions would all be answered, and in the mist of it all, that was incredibly exciting.

Back home, Aakil was a Doctor of Philosophy, once married, though she had passed several years ago, leaving him alone. He lived comfortably however, being the author of several best sellers and still delivering the occasional lecture at the university where he had worked for twenty years. However, here, on the hilltop, all of that meant nothing at all, and yet somehow, he liked himself more here, away from it all without any title or past accomplishment, loss or any of his possessions around him. In fact, he felt utterly exhilarated.

At the bottom of the hill, the lake glistened brighter now, the birds sang louder than before and this time, as the heat wrapped itself around him, he felt comforted by its warmth, and it was then that another wave of realisation swept through him.

Most of his pain had been brought on from the environment in which he lived, the baggage he carried around with him and the thoughts he had about it all, rather than the ailments themselves that were eating away at his physical being. The pain was hard to bear, but the fear of further suffering in that huge, empty house, all that time spent sat in his green-cushioned chair dwelling on past sorrows, grieving for his late wife, feeling anger at himself and his circumstances… feeling lonely. *That* was more painful; that was suffering at its most heightened state, and yet that suffering was within his power to control.

With closed eyes, Aakil took another deep inhale through his nose followed by a long exhale through his mouth. He repeated this over and over, until he felt he was there, in the right place, in the right state of being, where he was truly himself and at one with the universe.

Soft sounds of the river's gentle flow mixed with a beautiful birdsong, accompanied by the light breeze filled his ears; it was the most beautiful sound he'd ever heard - it was an orchestra in its most natural form. Golden rays of heat from the sun rest on his face, and it was there he found a moment of pure joy. A single tear ran down his cheek, this time from happiness, as he tapped into his own power, and as that tear fell onto the grass and went back into the Earth, Aakil realised that he was no longer lonely, for he saw just how connected to his surroundings he could be, how connected he was to it, right now, in this moment – *to all of it*.

A gentle smile formed on his crinkled face, for he felt no pain, no sickness, only peace and he wondered if he could perhaps stay here, on the hilltop, with the wildflowers, the glistening lake, the blue sky and the single red poppy by his side.

Oh No, Not Again
Chad Copley

Hi Chad
Oh no, not again! Tell us why we brought you here? Oh, we brought you here to see how you are. We hear you're poorly again, aren't you? You had a fight with a junior doctor. And he won't press charges if you admit that you are a danger to yourself and others.
Oh no, not again. You said you'd listen the last time.

Oh no, not again. Not you again.
All I know is I took the dog out at Aby's and when I got back there was an ambulance waiting to take me. Why can't I take the dog out?
Oh no, not again. It's every time I start to do things for myself and get my life back from the last time this happened.
Oh no, not again.

Oh no, not again.
You've got to stop this now.
This violence has got to stop
The doctor was just doing his job
He deserves better.
Chad, what were you thinking?
Tell the truth.
You're not treating anyone else like this,
I'll see to it. This has to stop.
Oh no, not again.

Oh no, not again.

When are you going to listen to anyone other than your team?

The doctor said I was ill and gave me 80 milligrams of Olandapine

And I ended up in hospital with deep vein thrombosis. I am accountable for my actions in everything, but he seems to be able to do and say anything with no consequence whatsoever.

It's happening again.
Oh no, not again.

Oh no, not again.
Chad, you have to see
We're not you're enemy
We're trying to help.
You just have to start to trust in our team and believe you will get better.
(Never again will you get the chance to hurt one of our team.)
Oh, no. Not again.

Why?
Come on, you bastards, tell me why this happens every time? I take my life back from being told how to think and feel.

I will be free
Of a doctor that read a file on me
I want a doctor, a proper doctor, to see me.
Oh no. Not again.

Oh no, not again.

Oh no, not again.
I believe I can achieve the life I need, deserve. And yes, I will be your consequence.

And I will fight for my life again.

Oh no, not again.

You say you want to be free, but you're not in any position… I mean, the right state of mind. You've been outwardly violent to staff, and we are first to take your rights away under the law. But you will see another doctor in the morning. And you will get your chance to put your point of view across.

But if it happens again like I know it will… it better not.
Oh no. Not again.

Oh. No. Not again.
You only see what you want to see.
I am not out of a text book
This is me, Chad Copley
Give me a proper doctor, who knows what they are doing
And the consequences for their actions.
It's my life now, and I make the rules. Oh no. Not again.

Never again.

The Dance
Lorna Weaver Dutton

In my white tutu, the cold mixes with the sun
on my bare shoulders. I'm wearing the dress with
hundreds of silver sequins, all sewed on by my mother.
The photographer gathers the cast in three rows.
Matching ballerinas, no more than six years old,
stand and sit around the village hall rockery,
smiling with their best fixed grins.

Now thirteen, I stand at the barre,
Feet at second position, arms in fourth, elegant.
The pianist accompanies our opening steps,
a jaunty melody at odds with our gentle movements.
Louise catches the teacher's eye with her natural poise,
While I coerce my limbs to follow directions.

At twenty-six, I transform myself from wedding white
to trampy red taffeta. He's less formal, changed from
the morning suit. But the real reveal won't appear
for years yet. We shuffle along to My Heart Will Go On,
in ignorant bliss of the shipwreck to come.

Black tap shoes on fifty-year-old heels and toes, protected by steel. I have progressed from novice to competent, more in sync with myself than ever.
The taps are the drums, the bodies drumsticks.
I'm finally dancing my way.

Miss Nicely and Friends
Virginia Sellar-Edmunds

Tears rolled down Morag McPherson's cheeks pooling at the bottom of her neck. How foolish she had been. Nothing would ever be the same again, she could now trust no one. She stifled a sob. A gentle arm went round her shoulders, and a tissue was pressed into her hand.

'Morag dear, whatever is the matter?' Letitia Nicely held her friend close in a gentle embrace.

'Oh Letty.' (Only Morag and Julia Johnston had the right to use the diminutive of Letitia's name.) 'I have been so foolish and now my comfortable life is in ruins.'

'What on earth do you mean?' enquired Miss Nicely. 'I'm sure things can't be that serious. Talk to me about it and we'll see what we can do to solve the problem.'

'I - It's like this,' Morag began. 'Yesterday I received a call claiming to be my bank. The caller said that there was a suspicion that my accounts had been used fraudulently, and that they needed me to transfer my money into a 'safe account.' They knew certain details about my accounts, and I was convinced that I was doing the right thing. I transferred all my holdings into the said account and gave them authority to work on my original accounts. When I phoned the bank this morning to see what was happening, it became clear that I'd been caught by a cruel scam. All my money is gone - both from my current account and my savings too.'

'How much are we talking about dear? I know that that is an indelicate question, but it may help me to know.'

'Over £100,000 in my savings, and about £2,000 in my current account.'

The only sign of emotion in Miss Nicely was a pursing

of the lips and a slight frown. She had taught herself not to react visibly, but she felt things deeply, most particularly unfairness. Morag's case was one that affected her more than many. Not only the unfairness of it, but because she was one of the two friends who mattered most to her. It was long established that she had control of 'the body' on a Wednesday morning between the hours of five to ten till five past twelve. That was the time that she met Morag and Julia without fail. But it meant that time was running out.

Miss Nicely pondered a plan. As an elderly superhero she thought she knew who would help with it. Her much younger alter-ego Vixen LeStrange would just have to wait to regain control of the body today.

'Morag dear, I have a plan. I can't tell you what it is, as it is slightly less than legal, but I'm sure that if you stay here Julia will look after you, until you are calm enough to go home again,'

'Of course, I will,' said Julia emphatically. She had remained silent till now, recognising that the conversation needed to be between her two friends, but she had listened intently to what was being said and was livid on behalf of Morag. 'Go on Letty, and see what can be done!'

Miss Nicely's faithful steed – a flying sit-up-and-beg bicycle named Pegasus, with an old-fashioned wicker basket – was straining at his bike lock waiting for Letitia to climb aboard and direct him to where she wanted to go.

Pegasus was the perfect form of transport for an elderly superhero. To all appearances, Miss Nicely was a strait-laced elderly lady, with all the good habits of a thoughtful cyclist. She always looked before she pulled out and gave clear hand signals. She made sure to ride in cycle lanes and to respect road signs. Of course she didn't spend much time on the roads, but still…

Smoothing her sensible coat, and making sure that the

laces of her sturdy brogues were tied, Miss Nicely mounted Pegasus and said, 'Let's go then.'

Glasgow was the direction that Pegasus was turned towards. He knew the way well and needed no directions to the disused docks where Angus Bulman, a former Aberdonian criminal, aka the Hairy Coo, transacted his business. As Pegasus landed, Angus sauntered across the yard to greet them.

'Well, hello, you old baggage,' was Angus's greeting.

'Good day dear,' began Miss Nicely. 'It's nice to see you too. Is there any chance of a spot of penitence today? No? Then that's all to the good for me.'

'Well, how then?' asked a startled Hairy Coo.

'I have a little job for which you are the very man. Your various nefarious activities put you in an advantageous position to help me.'

'Well, how's that then?'

'I need you to find me some criminals and bring them here for a meeting with me. It would be most unseemly if I were to chase them down myself, as I haven't been physically alerted to the crime. I know of it on a personal level, as it affects one of my dearest friends.'

Miss Nicely brought the Hairy Coo up to speed on the details of the criminals, and asked if he would be so obliging as to fetch them to his office, where she would be ready to meet them and deal with them forthwith.

'Well... aye... I'd be delighted... to help,' stuttered Angus. In spite of his apparent disdain for Miss Nicely, he was really quite fond of the 'old busybody'.

'Thank you, dear,' was Letitia's fervent response.

'Well, I'll be in touch.' Angus dismissed her, walking back across the muddy yard to his office, pondering a plan which would never be divulged to a living soul.

Miss Nicely was prepared to have to wait for a while before

the Hairy Coo could oblige her, so she was pleasantly surprised to be messaged in his own inimitable way – with the commission of a crime serious enough to warrant Miss Nicely's intervention (let us just say that kidnap was involved) after just 48 hours. She was already in Miss Nicely mode when the call arrived, so she finished off her assigned task with indecorous speed – the miscreant got only the phase one light admonishment, rather than the full monty stage three chastisement, which he most definitely deserved.

Settling onto Pegasus's saddle, Miss Nicely turned his handlebars and rearing excitedly he set off for Glasgow.

Pegasus understood that this was an important appointment and made haste. Having made good time, they were banking and turning towards the yard used by Angus Bulman, a.k.a. the Hairy Coo, as the epicentre of his criminal activities. He had come up against Miss Nicely several times in the past and she harboured great hopes of him having an epiphany and cleaning up his act. She felt bad having used his criminality to assist her in the present crisis over Morag's financial losses. The ends would hopefully justify the means.

As Pegasus and his rider alighted in the well-known yard, the Hairy Coo came out of the Portacabin that he used as his office, and across the yard to meet them.

'Well,' he began as was his wont, 'I've got the low lives that you wanted. I made sure to get the two criminal 'master minds' who were responsible for scamming your friend. Mind you, there's plenty to choose from.'

'Thank you, Angus dear,' replied Miss N. 'I will be forever grateful to you for your prompt assistance.'

'Well, they're in the office, handcuffed to each other as well as to the chairs. They're going nowhere until you've finished with them.'

'Goodness,' replied Miss Nicely. 'You've obviously taken all necessary precautions,'

'Well, they're a shifty pair right enough, and I wouldn't put it past them to flit.'

'I'd like to see them now, I think.' She set off to the office, escorted by the Hairy Coo.

'Well, I'll stay on guard out here,' said Angus. 'You go in and deal with your business.'

Miss Nicely entered the office. Two sulky, furious men sat handcuffed to each other, and to the chairs just as the Hairy Coo described.

'Right my dears,' began Letitia. 'I know you will have swindled people extensively, but I'm here to deal with one scam in particular. It took place on Tuesday last week and concerns a very dear friend of mine, Miss Morag McPherson. You swindled her out of her life savings, as well as the contents of her current account and it just won't do.'

One of the men sneered at her and said, 'I remember her – she was an easy mark. Swallowed our story lock, stock and smoking barrel. People like her are just asking to be swindled.'

Miss Nicely pulled herself up to her full 5' 3'.

'No dear,' in her most impressively stern tones. Her voice became dangerously sharp, and her eyes flashed like steel.

'No one deserves to be scammed into losing their security, whoever they are. If you make full restitution to Morag and to as many of your other victims as possible, then this once I will refrain from handing you over to the local constabulary to be charged and then sent before the magistrates to be remanded in custody ahead of a county court hearing.'

The man who had sneered at her, now asked, 'What's in it for you? I assume you want a cut of the cash?'

'No, dear,' replied Miss Nicely, quite horrified by the

suggestion, shifting her weight uncomfortably from one foot to the other. 'I just wish to see my friend and others like her, recompensed and see you using your undoubted social skills in an honest manner.'

The apparent spokesman started to grumble about the difficulties facing them but was stopped by Miss Nicely who was still in full and insistent serious admonishment mode.

'No dear – I don't want to hear your complaints. I just want justice for my friend Miss McPherson, and as many other people as you can deal with. Am I quite clear?' This was said in very impressive tones that brooked no disagreement.'

There was some more grumbling as the criminals discussed the order and then the spokesman nodded.

'Very well – my associate will release you, but have no fear – if I find that you haven't made reparations there will be consequences that you can only imagine.'

Miss Nicely left the 'office' and instructed the Hairy Coo to let the scammers go, but to keep a subtle eye on them till further notice.

The following Wednesday at 10.00 sharp, Letitia was waiting for her friends in the café. They came in together having met in the street. Morag looked like a different person from the week before. Beaming, she said, 'Oh Letty, I don't know how you did it, but all my money has been returned apart from £20 which had been spent on fish and chips.'

'Dear Letty, thank you for whatever you did to deal with Morag's plight. It is good to know that we have a friend like you to sort seemingly intractable problems for us.' Julia embraced Miss Nicely briefly and then said, 'Now let's order our coffee and I think that we should all have a cream cake in celebration.'

Northern Lights
William Davidson

You wake me after midnight to say the Northern Lights are dancing across the sky. I ask you if the kettle's on. You say they are solar winds blowing from the Sun. I stagger to the kitchen and brew a pot of Yorkshire tea. You talk about clouds of particles. I pour two cups and add four sugars to mine. You step out into the garden and say they are green and red because the oxygen is excited. I open a packet of Hobnobs. You raise your arms like you're waving off a friend. I dunk a biscuit.

Mermaid
Yeti Hammond

I caught a glimpse in the witching hour,
Of scales that silver shone,
Flick of a tail in the pale moonlight,
Then all sight was gone.

Cold seeping in my bones
I will not take your hand

Because I know you'll drag me down,
Down into the crushing waters,
Where light and colours cannot reach,
You're gonna drag me down,
Down into the crushing waters,
Where you will be the end of me.

I watch the shore for a sight of you,
Even as the Spring storms rage,
Your haunting song entrances me,
As it floats across the waves

Blood rushing in my ears
I reach to take your hand

'though I know you'll drag me down,
Down into the crushing waters,
Where light and colours cannot reach,
And now I'm sinking down,
Down into the crushing waters,
Where you will be the end of me.

Dark filling up my soul
I hold onto your hand

Even as you drag me down,
Down into the crushing waters,
Where light and colours cannot reach,
Now you've dragged me down,
Down into the crushing waters,
Where you will be the end of me.

This poem can also be sung. The chords are:

Verse
C G Am F   x2
Pre Chorus
Am G D G
Chorus
C G Am F   x2

Chicken Bones
Gemma Fawcett

Belinda set up her own business with her friend Jan called 'Lollipops'. The idea behind the business was that children's clothes parties were held at people's houses and the host would earn a commission on the sales and of course most of the money went to Lollipops. Kind of what would be referred to as a pop-up shop nowadays. The clothes were bought for cheap from warehouses in Bradford which were heavily marked up by the duo. Sometimes unknowingly they picked out product ahead of trend. For example buying kids pyjamas on the theme of Gladiators before it exploded in popularity in the 90's. When it went mainstream sales of Gladiators pyjamas skyrocketed. Initially the parties started with their individual contacts and friends which then spread by word of mouth. These kinds of parties were quite popular in the 90's and was a good income stream for the pair – certainly beat working for a few quid an hour. On a good night they would pocket £100. Ten-year-old Freya, Belinda's daughter, would help her mum with the business, writing receipts and folding clothes – this gave her a bit of pocket money and mum avoided the cost of a babysitter. About five doors down from their home was a lady called Liz who was Sadie & Kurt's mum – they held a party once there. They owned a few pitbull dogs who absolutely stunk. The entire house smelled of Dog. After some time in the house you would come out smelling like a mutt. After the party Belinda and Freya were quick to pack up the stock lest it picked up the hideous smell. When home Belinda proactively sprayed the stock with Frebreze.

Another day they went to the house which Freya referred to as the 'chicken palace'. Another smelly house, Freya sat next to an elderly lady called Ethel on a corduroy sofa in the living room. The elderly lady was wearing a pleated tweed skirt and a short-sleeved blouse and had very deep wrinkles on her face showing a life well lived. Ethel was blathering on about 'Tax' (Freya did not know what that was). The old lady repeatedly talked about them being 'robbing bastards'. She told Freya, 'I flatly refuse to pay the robbing bastards'. I much prefer the supposed punishment. It's like a little jolly for me. I can't afford a holiday, but jail feels like a holiday.'

For many years she had dodged the tax man and flatly refused to pay. Not paying taxes is one of the few financial misdemeanours which holds a prison sentence. Ethel harked on about how she enjoyed her 'holidays' at HMP New Hall. She said, 'Pretty much every year I get sent to New Hall and I have made some friends there that are on longer sentences. It's fun.' Ethel saved money by being provided with 3 meals a day and a comfy wipe down bed which is somewhat handy when pissing the bed was a regular occurrence. She would only really get a few weeks at a time – sometimes days but she looked forward to them and genuinely thought of them as holidays. With her hand slightly in line with her face Ethel motioned indicating that there was some kind of secret to tell. While Belinda was leaning towards Ethel her hand slipped down the crack between the cushions of the sofa. Her hand hit upon something hard which after a quick feel Belinda fished out. There appeared a half-eaten, mouldy chicken bone with one of those long thin bone fragments. Freya would never eat KFC in her lifetime.

Illustration by Gemma Fawcett

The Magick Wand
L.D. Ethrae

Once upon a time, there was a girl whose village was under attack by bandits. The girl, being urged by her father to go in search of a mystical branch that could cast mighty spells to save the village, began to climb the mountain upon which it was said to grow. On the ascent, she was met by three mysterious entities.

The first, a cloaked man, offered her a short-cut through a dark tunnel. The girl was tempted at first, but then looked into the tunnel, and saw all manner of unsettling things inside it, including skeletons. The girl backed away, but the cloaked stranger said she could make it through unscathed if she paid the price. The girl asked about the dead – the stranger said they refused to pay him before entering and therefore failed in their quest. The girl asked what the price was. The cloaked man answered that it was a third of her heart. The girl, seeing there was some light at the end of the tunnel, knew the way through was short, but knew that without her heart whole she would not care to use the wand to save her people. She refused, and climbed the mountain higher.

The second entity was a golden snake, who guarded a shining lake of water. The girl was very thirsty from the climb and a good swimmer, and the Wand lay a short way across the lake, up a small hill. The snake said she could drink from it and cross to get the wand, if she paid the price. She looked into the lake to see many drowned people. The snake said they did not pay him, and so paid with their lives. She asked what the price was. The snake answered that it was a third of her memories. She refused, knowing that without her memories, she would forget to save her people. She continued up the mountain, going around the lake.

The third and final entity was a female Giant who was heavy with child. She caressed her stomach and offered to hoist the girl up the final wall. The girl, knowing it must come at a price, inquired as to what it would cost. The Giant said it would come at no price, that she knew how it felt to want to save those for whom you cared. The girl looked around the base of the wall and saw no bodies, but saw nail marks on the rock. At the same time, she wondered how the Giant knew of her quest. The girl, not fooled by the lying Giant, began to climb on her own, despite being tired. The Giant then stood up to try and stop the girl, revealing a pile of bones where she had been sitting. But the girl used the last of her strength and, having become good at climbing after taking the hard way up, was too small and fast. The Giant cried, saying she had to eat, or her baby would be born sickly. The girl wept when she was on the top of the wall, and promised she would use the Wand to help the Giant get food. The girl stumbled on and came at last to the tree upon which the Wand grew. The tree offered her the Wand, but said it was good for only one spell and that the desires, and the souls, of those who had fallen in attempt to get it were its source of power. Using a spell would free their souls and it would take many hundreds more souls to charge it. The girl had neither the time, nor the heart, to kill people for their souls and desires. She had to choose – save her village from bandits, or the Giant and her baby from starvation, to both of whom she had given her word. The girl, determined to save both, cast her one spell. She wished for those suffering near the mountain to be saved.

The Giant was magically transported down the mountain and gorged on the bandits that were killing the girl's people. In gratitude, the Giant returned to the mountain and left the girl and her people in peace. The girl, however, became racked with grief witnessing the power of the Wand recharge with the spirits of the bandits. She had kept her heart, her memories and her body, but now felt as though she had lost her soul.

She grasped the Wand tight and snapped it in two.

Fantasy Tutorial:
How to Form a Party
Junior Mark Cryle

Hi, I'm Cryle Monroe. You might remember me from such tutorials as 'Zombie Apocalypse Survival Guide', 'Didgery-Do's and Don'ts from Down Under' and 'How to Train your Demon Lord's Chief Eunuch'.

Today's session is a must-know for all you fantasy enthusiasts, and a popular trope in many stories within the genre: How to form your Party (For how to throw a party, please proceed to Party Planning 101, next door on your left).

Now, a Party is a group of Adventurers or skilled individuals, and the acting POV in your tale. Typically.

Topic #1: Party Size.

This refers to the number of characters you have in it.

For beginners of the trope, I'd recommend two characters to start with, but no more than four. With some experience you can try up to eight characters. Once you're confident enough then you can try with nine characters and more.

Multiple character interactions can lead to interesting story elements, but too many can be tricky to juggle if you get carried away.

Think of yourself as a Dungeon Master for a TTRPG (Table Top Role Playing Game): two or three players is easier to manage than eight, both in and out of the game, so just keep that in mind and you'll be fine.

Well, mostly fine.

Maybe.

Topic #2a: Party Roles.

Like performers in the world of theatre, everyone has a part to play which benefits the party in many ways. For simplicity, I'll elaborate on four of the most common roles you may find in Fantasy Adventure Stories.

First, the Tank: they can take a hit while protecting their allies and hit back harder.

Next, the Healer: the ones that keeps the party alive and healthy on the campaign, with or without magic.

Then there's the Controller who controls aspects of a battlefield, be it the environment or the enemies' numbers.

And then you have the Face who deals with the negotiations and social interactions that some may struggle with. Not all Fantasy tales have to have epic fights for the heroes to claim victory.

While it is possible for a character to play multiple roles, and there are many to choose from, like with Topic #1 it can be overwhelming if carried away.

For those starting off, I'd recommend defined roles (one per character), then you can explore flexible roles (defined, but capable of other tasks), even well-rounded roles once you're confident enough (The jack-of-all-trades of fantasy).

Of course, as the heading hinted, roles go hand in hand with;

Topic #2b: Party Classes (AKA Jobs).

These help to determine what roles are open to a character and what path you wish to take their development on. Because, as much as we deny it, no one is good at everything (You know who you are, I see you hiding).

Using the example roles from before, let's explore the classes that are commonly paired with them.

Tanks usually take the form of the Warrior, well-armoured and armed for combat, stereotypically the first to fight (which is not a bad thing at times).

Controller is suited for a Mage, for in a world of swords and sorcery their magic can thin the enemy numbers or alter the terrain to suit the needs of the Party, but a Strategist may play the same role if you prefer a non-magical adventure.

For your Healer needs you'd get no better than a Cleric, they've gone hand in hand for decades, despite the religious themes they'd introduce (touchy subject).

For the Face, none suit the role better than the Bard, these musical storytellers are the best in social circles as they've been around and would naturally know how to draw a crowd (think tour guides, the melodramatic ones).

Classes can branch off into subclasses, leading to more diverse roles and more story possibilities, but for now please stick to one class and one role per character, until you're experienced and confident enough to experiment.

Less is more in this case, especially to avoid an early burnout (not literally).

Finally the last and, given today's mindsets, potentially controversial;

Topic #3: Party Races. Hear me out.

In the context of storytelling, particularly Fantasy and Sci-Fi, Races add not only world building to beef up your tale, but also to party composition because, in all honesty, some races are better suited to certain roles and classes than others.

Let's look at, what I affectionately refer to as, the Triad of Fantasy: a Trio of the most recurring and prominent races in any Fantasy adventure, magical or not.

You have Humans, typically your main POV, who are often the most numerous, diverse and versatile species. They are fiction's Jack-of-all-trades with no outstanding traits or qualities. Usually.

Then there's Elves, with the longest longevity of the three. They are attuned to nature, fast and dexterous, but often lack social etiquette due to their secluded lifestyles, to the point of even looking down at those with shorter lifespans.

And lastly the Dwarves, the hardy and bearded people of short stature from the mountains (usually). What they lack in speed and grace they make up with strength and work know-how.

Each adds different story elements if used correctly, and there are a multitude of races within this genre, with the addition of mixed races that add even more layers of storytelling. But, as before, best to leave this mountain alone until you've gained the skills and confidence required. Beginners should stick to single-raced characters for simplicity.

Bonus Topic; For the Experimentalists (yes, you).

If you've written fantasy prior, it can get repetitive at times, especially with your Party builds. That's why I'll demonstrate a randomised prompt-generating method for such an occasion, with a tried and true RPG tool.

Dice. Six-sided, eight-sided, four-sided, and the iconic twenty-sided too.

First, a D-20 to determine the party size I have to work with.

clink, rattle Make a note of that.

Next, a D-8 for Role quantity, followed by a D-6 for Classes. You can work better around multi-roles than multi-classes, as the latter lacks compatible combinations.

clink, rattle That's one.

clink, rattle And two.

Finally, one more roll of the D-6 for Race quantity. On average, diversity is more of a seasoning than a necessity.

clink,rattle Interesting.

In order, I've rolled Six, Six, Five and One.

Which means I can form a Party of six characters, with six roles and five classes between them with two members sharing a class, and one race to work with. Meaning, I could have a gang of Humans, a group of Dwarves, or a band of Elves.

Honestly, it's one of my better set of results. Last month, I got One, Six, Six, and Five.

That's right; One Adventurer with six roles, five classes, and a mixed culture of five Races.

Pray your first rolls are kinder to you.

That concludes today's Tutorial. Join me next time as we explore the wonderful world of Romance and why my wife left me for a ninja cyborg werewolf. I'm not bitter. Not at all!

ahem Class dismissed. Excuse me.

…Now, where's that silver plasma bullet I bought on eBay?

Illustration by Stephanie Jardine

Home
Carol Coffey

Home, how I do love home
We have bad days and even worse days, screaming and shouting, violence, fights, tit for tat
but home is my happy place

Home, how I do love home
We laugh, we celebrate, we smile, rejoice
home is my happy place

Home, how I do love home
Troubled teenagers, howling dogs and their accidents on the floors,
Fear, loss, cleaning, anger, pain and even more pain,
but home is my happy place

Home is my very best friend - keeps me dry from the rain, warm from the cold, shaded from the sun,
sheltered from the storms and blustery days

Oh I do love home
Home is so my happy place

Home, I love you – you, maybe at Dad's, Tamar's, the

Coffey fold

Wherever you are that day, that week, that month, that year,
I do love home, my very best happy place

We go to France, USA, or even Spain, but wherever I go I want you, home
Home is so my happy place

So now I know that I will always miss home, my happy place

Where I married, had endless friends, family, kids around
From Christenings to birthday parties, sleepless tiring nights
whether it's breastfeeding or waiting for your child to return home from a
Sleep over or drinking party
Home is my very best happy place

My home has always had a lot of drama, various sufferings, trauma, diagnoses, a lot to deal with
But home is truly my happy place

When I think of home I think stress, migraines, pain, but I still want to go home - how addictive you are
Home is my happy place

Home, how I dread going there today.   I really, really do.
But I do love you home
Somehow, I must find the strength today and everyday
Just another mountain to climb
I will get there to you, home

My home, my very best happy place

A Coach Driver's Day
Catherine Pemberton

Mark had just a few more pick-ups to make before taking his passengers to the coast for the day. When he had picked everyone up, he introduced himself and told them what to do in an emergency. The journey should take no longer than two hours depending on the traffic he said. They got on their way.

The passengers started to chat with each other.

It wasn't long before one passenger shouted, 'Are we there yet!?'

After seeing a sign for the coast, Mark said, 'No, not quite.'

Then a few miles later the same passenger saw another sign and shouted, 'Are we there yet!?'

Once again Mark shouted, 'No, not quite!'

'You said that before,' she shouted.

'I will let you all know when we are nearly there,' Mark shouted back. 'Just sit back, relax and enjoy the journey.'

The rest of the passengers continued chatting.

After a few more miles the passenger saw another sign for the coast, but Mark went another way.

'Stop. You're going the wrong way!' she shouted.

Mark shouted back, 'No we aren't. I have done this trip many times and this is the way I always go.'

He thought to himself, 'We have a right one here – maybe I should let her do the driving.'

After another few outbursts they soon arrived and got dropped off near the beach.

'I will pick you up from here at 4:30 prompt,' Mark told them.

They all got off the bus and started to go their own way

except the woman who did all the shouting. She was left on her own.

'This is as far as you go, love,' he said to the passenger.

'Are you staying here?' she asked.

' No,' said Mark. 'I am going to park the bus about a mile out of town, then go and visit a friend.'

'Are you going through the town?'

'Well, not really. Where do you want to go?'

'Not sure where I want to be,' she said.

'Tell you what,' said Mark, 'I will drop you off in town then you might be able to find your own way back to the beach! Is that ok?'

The woman looked a bit blank and said, 'Yes, ok.'

He dropped her off near Robert's Coffee House and went on his way.

The rest of the passengers had an enjoyable day; some went paddling in the sea, others sat on the sand eating picnic lunches then spent a few hours walking round town and visiting coffee shops.

When it got to pick-up time all the passengers were there except one. Mark asked them if they had seen her. No one had. He said he had dropped her off near Robert's Coffee House.

'Oh, we went in there,' said a couple. 'We didn't see her. Maybe someone ought to go and look for her.'

The bus waited for ten minutes. No sight of her. They drove slowly down the sea front but still no sight of her.

Mark thought, 'Just my luck.'

He decided to drive to the shopping area and sent a couple to look for her. They visited the coffee shops and the other shops on both sides of the street. No one had seen her.

At this point Mark was starting to get a bit worried. He rang Jim, his boss, to find out what he should do.

'How long has she been missing for?' Jim asked.

'I dropped her off in town at about eleven am,' said Mark. 'No one has seen her since. Just wondered what I should do.'

'Do you have her name and contact details on your passenger list?' asked Jim.

'Have her name, no details,' replied Mark.

'Think the best thing to do is go back and do another sweep of the sea front, then get in touch with the police. If you give me her name I will find her details, then I can go from there.'

The police were informed, and Mark took the rest of his passengers home.

It was a worrying time for him as in a way he felt responsible for his passengers.

After a few hours' search the police had found a woman of her description sitting on a seat in a church yard.

'Hello, is your name Doris?' asked the policewoman.

'Yes,' she said, sounding rather upset.

'What are you doing here?'

'Talking to my husband; he is sat beside me,' said Doris.

'So he is. It's getting cold and dark; don't you think it's time to go home?' said the policewoman.

Doris said, 'No, my place is here with my Fred.'

By this time her son and daughter-in-law had been found and were on their way.

'Have you had anything to eat today, Doris?' asked the policewoman.

'Not since I had my breakfast,' Doris replied.

'Are you feeling hungry?' asked the policewoman.

'Yes, just a bit; I could do with a cup of tea as well,' Doris said.

'You say goodbye to Fred, then we will go and get you

somewhere warm and some food.'

Doris got up off the seat with tears rolling down her face and was taken back to the police station. She was put in the interview suite, made comfortable and given something to eat and drink.

It was a few hours later when her son and daughter-in-law arrived.

'Thank goodness she is safe,' her son Dan said. His wife June went to see Doris. She was sleeping.

The police wanted to know why she was out on her own in her condition.

Dan said he knew there was something not quite right with Mum but didn't think it was this bad.

'How did she lose her husband?' asked the policewoman.

'He died from complications following a heart operation,' said Dan.

'How long ago?'

'Coming up to four years,' Dan replied.

'Were his ashes scattered in the sea?' enquired the policewoman.

'No, he is buried in our home church yard. Why?' Dan asked.

'She was found sitting in a church yard talking to him,' said the policewoman.

'Oh,' said Dan rather surprised. 'What was the church called?'

'St. Marks,' the policewoman replied.

'I'm not sure,' Dan said, 'I think it might be the name of a church where they got married.'

By this time Doris and June were reunited with Dan. 'Thank you for all you have done for her,' he said.

'You need to keep a close eye on her,' said the policewoman.

Dan and June agreed and went home.

That next morning when Mark turned up for work, he asked Jim if the missing woman had been found.

'Yes, safe and well – just a bit confused.'

Mark hoped today was going to be a better day.

The Fall
Glenne Shearer

Heading to the end of my street at a near run, last minute as usual and afraid I'd miss the bus, I went flying.

Man on a bicycle. Grey beard. Brown coat. Would he stop? Concrete. Sky. Pain. Confusion. Quiet. Time. He must have gone past.

The man's face loomed over me. Relief. Gratitude. And an almost imperceptible disappointment. It had begun to feel peaceful lying there, contemplating the blue and white above me.

I grasped the hand he offered and as he pulled, he staggered. Dead weight. Perhaps he would end up on top of me, a very confusing sight for any other passer-by. Not what you'd expect on Bishy Rd on a Wednesday morning.

I raised my other hand. He braced himself and with both hands managed to pull me off the ground.

Thank you, thank you. How did I manage to do that? He pointed out the slight dip in the angle of the corner. I must have mis-stepped, the weight of my rucksack propelling me forward, no time to steady myself.

Are you OK?

Well, I don't seem to have broken anything, I said, flexing my arms and legs. I could feel the impact on my right hip, dark bruises ready to form, shock waves rippling up my spine, trip hazard warnings for the elderly running through my head. Be More Careful.

You did it right, he said. You rolled.

I had! I had rolled. I had repressed the instinct to put my arms out, afraid they might shatter. I had made myself go limp and roll when I hit the ground. I had thwarted disaster.

I had fallen. Falling. It felt like a metaphor. Falling through the net. Falling out of favour. Falling from grace. Falling away from myself and this world.

There are times when I'd be happy to leave the world, but I'd like it to be in a quiet, peaceful way. Nodding off in my chair, in front of an episode of Countdown, my breath slowing as the Countdown clock ticks off the seconds, last words fading away as I fall through the veil from this world to another.

Not the indignity of a spectacular fall, spreadeagled on the ground in full view of the neighbours.

It was very dramatic, he had said. Pity I couldn't have got it on camera.

Going to the Zoo
Keith Myers

My friend and I take a trip to the zoo.
We hear tropical birds as they coo.
Zebras graze and monkeys make a noise in their cage,
Lions roar nearby in a rage,
Elephants and their young ones rest in the enclosure eating their greens,
Hippos nearby get a wash, splashing about so it seems.
Further on flamingos some pink,
Gracefully walking round in a link.
Walking on, we see wolves prowling round,
Waiting on every sound,
Tigers roam and take it in,
Paddling round with kith and kin.
Walking on, we see a sign for snakes,
Reptiles in cages whatever it takes,
Grass snakes and longer ones like cobras and anacondas worm around.
Odd hiss but not much sound.
There are turtles and climbing insects about.
We wander out and look for a time out,
Get a coffee and scone,
Feel better after it's done.
We stroll to a theme park,

The rides look scary, the water screams with make believe sharks.

Looking round we go on a train ride and maybe a log flume.

Perhaps there are dodgem rides, give us some room.

So let's finish with an ice cream.

Licking away, we sum up the pleasant day we have had, what a team.

Taking a stroll on the paths and out of the zoo,

The weather has been good and so we are too.

Illustration by Stephanie Jardine

Tick Tock

Christina

Tick tock, Tick tock, Tick tock

The sound of a swing pendulum clock, it's all I can hear… tick tock, tick tock, tick tock.

As I lay here I can't feel my legs, arms, body they seem to be unmoveable. I don't seem to have my eyes or mouth covered, am I blinking? I don't know? It's dark as death wherever I am plus there's a strange, odd smell like fresh cut flower, damp earth from my potting shed (weird how do I know I've got a potting shed) it feels cold and cave like. As I lay here at least I think I'm laying down.

Am I buried or in a box I don't think so as there seems to be a flow of air across my face I shiver, tick tock, my mind seems to jar to life. Why are you being so calm it screams at me, I try to shrug but, my body doesn't seem to move, a wave of something hits me - adrenalin, I think? I start to gag oh god I think I can't move I don't want to choke to death, sweat starts to pore out of me and all the time in the background I can hear tick tock, tick tock, suddenly a rhyme pops into my head, *'The mouse runs up the clock,'* I say out loud, I think. I hear a quiet snigger far away, I whisper 'Hello?' Nothing, absolutely nothing.

Tick tock, tick tock, tick tock.

My mind shouts what the hell's going on…
I think I shout back 'I DON'T KNOW' again. I hum part of a rhyme *'goes my grandfather's clock'*.

Tick tock, tick tock, tick tock.

I drift, I don't know for how long, I'm feeling strange woozy, like I'm floating in the air. Wake up, my mind is saying, over and over. It's quite annoying and still I hear the rhythmic beat of a clock.

Fluctuating in and out of consciousness my mind has stopped shouting at me. It seems to have reverted to our childhood. Sometimes it sings a rhyme.

Hickory, dickory, dock… Hay diddle, diddle the cat and the fiddle. Very, very slowly I say:
'If all the world was-s-s paaaper-r-r…' I'm off again.

Tick tock, tick tock, tick tock.

Pain real goddamn pain, I think I'm screaming really loud, real pain.
My brain is on fire, the pain unbearable; it feels like a million ants are eating it. I'm sure if I could use my eyes I'd be crying, calling out - maybe I am?

Sharp pain I'm back…
'And all the seas are ink and all the trees are bread and cheese what would we have to drink.'
All I hear is a growling noise coming from my mouth but at least I think I can feel that moving and of course…

Tick tock, pain, tick tock, pain, again, again and again.

I dream I'm sitting in a glass house. I can feel the sun on my face. A few days earlier I'd potted a few sunflowers and begonias. I'm looking at what's supposed to be a begonia but something else is growing rapidly. I think it's looking at me; it's got huge for something that was only planted on Wednesday. Normally there wouldn't even be a stub for a few weeks but it's now at least three feet high like something from the day of the triffids.

There's that smell again, more pain, more drifting…

Tick tock tick tock, tick tock.

I drift back into consciousness. I'm feeling more awake at this moment the most I've felt in ages. I've noticed something else: I don't know whether it's in my mind or real but I'm sure I can see a cursor flicking in the lower corner of my right eye. In the darkness behind my eyes I can see little red insects whizzing around and around.

The weirdest thing is happing to me: my memories are being downloaded like flashing pictures of my past, deleted like lines of data no longer required… I want them, they're mine, faster and faster, it's happening.

'Stop, stop they're mine, my memories!'

'Hello, is there anyone there help me, stop this please!'

Nothing.

'PLEASE!'

I drift again as my life as a baby disappears into blankness. I lay like a shell feeling nothing, still the curser is blinking.
I'm cold, hot, shivering, cool, warm, drifting in and out still no sight, movement or feeling in my body. How do I know that?

You don't.

Tick tock, tick tock, Tick tock.

I'm in thick tar trying to move but it's hard. I'm waiting for something to happen. I haven't heard a solitary sound other than the clock. Not even sure I really heard the snigger.
'What's a snigger?'
I lay without movement, without anything, just blankness.

I think I see movement in the corner of my right eye near where I thought I saw the cursor.
'Why do I know that name?' I ask myself.
There's a ringing in my head but I don't know why. A buzzing, like the drone of a bee.
'What's a bee?'
Questions, questions, questions. Perhaps they didn't take everything from my mind.
Tick tock, tick tock…
'Oh, sod off,' I say.

Suddenly I hear click, click, click, over, over and over again, like someone is standing clicking their fingers.
'Who are you? What are you doing to me?'

I see movement to my right, but instead of the little red ants, it's blue, slightly larger than the red ants, behind my eyes, it's on its own.
'If it's you causing the buzzing in my head, please stop it now.'
Nothing.

I don't think I am drifting anymore. It's more like I'm being switched off and on. There's no wooziness, no pain, just darkness, awareness and repeat. I'm at an all-time low, weeping, shouting, trying to find something to say. Nothing seems to be the normal. Suddenly, pain, unbearable pain, I hear the clicking of fingers. I panic screaming, screaming.

'Why-y-y-y?' I shout. Blackness descends.

Tick tock, tick tock, tick tock.

'Ouch.' No real pain but what felt like a quick mild shock to the brain. Was I out for quite some time? It feels cold and damp again. The smell. The smell is back again.

Here comes the blue ant in the corner of my eye; it has multiplied, there are now three of them. I'm not sure if I'm imagining it, but I think I can somehow hear a whispering, but it's so low I can't make it out. Have I become so disillusioned that I want to hear the blue ants talking to me? Or come to that, anyone or anything talking to me.

'I can't hear you,' I say.
'Turn the volume up.'
Buzzing, buzzing. A squeaking noise, quite loud, making my teeth grate together and, all of a sudden, I hear a sound which turns into a rather rude electronic voice.
'*Shut up now. If the red ones hear you, we'll be destroyed.*'
'How rude! Ouch.'
'*Next time it will be worse.*'
I make a little sound before I can speak. Zap. I take a deep breath. I say in my head, okay, okay, you win.
'*Thank you. If you feel the red ones coming, say something.*'
I say this in my head, 'reds to the left, reds to the left.'
The blues disappear so quick I think I'm imagining it. The reds ants are all over the place now. Blackness.

I keep getting shocked in and out of awareness. The blue

ants have returned at last. I'm silent hoping they'll stay.

'We are ready. After we have shown you what is going on, you will sleep for a long time, as not everything is ready. It has taken longer than we thought as the reds keep destroying us and the information we're trying to save for you. Thank God it is now stored safely.'

I'm silent, worried that they will go if I talk.
You may speak.
'What are you going to show me?'
You will see.
'Better if you tell me first, please.'
NO… now we will show you very quickly what you are at the moment.
'What do you mean, at the moment?'

A flash of light appears. I stare ahead (pardon the pun you'll understand why). There, in a jar to my right, are my eyes; to my left is my mouth; and in the middle is my brain, all connected by wires, attached to three bell jars with liquid in. That must be the viscus feeling. My eyes are popping out like a cartoon character's eyes on springs. My mouth is screaming but there's no noise. As for my brain, it looks like it's shaking like a blancmange just tipped out of a tin.

This all happens in a few seconds. Suddenly I shout, 'Red ants! Red ants!' But the blue ants are already gone. As I drift again, the last thing that enters my mind is, Where were my ears? And all that's left is…

Tick tock, tick tock, tick tock.

The Home of New Beginnings
Dawn Skelton

A shimmering bright directive delight, internal peaceful ownership accustomed to healing.
A quest of self-discovery, secure sensitive aspirations, in the wealth of intimate silence.
The journey of unexplained solitude, a safe place in communicative literate escape.

An era universally inspired, in richness, my narrative vocation.
A storyteller, proclaimed in vulnerability, 'My Voice', echoed in illustrated acceptance.
Excited ventures, divulging 'New Beginnings to a New Dawn', unearthing breakthroughs.
Sharpened senses, self-enquiry, my daring notion purposefully presented.
A gallery of sentiments, memories, forthright, bold, chronicles courageously unfold, told.

Held in watchfulness, eagerly shifting through an extraordinary revolutionary forecast.
The sandstorm clearing, I witness inner landscapes, in self-belief, a responsive formation.

Milestones awaken, a route to merging wholeness, I go
well, steady, sturdy, strong.
A floral bloom, the origin of seasonal fluorescent growth,
marking a miraculous mystery.
Dreamlike ambitions in a welcomed terrain
to my internal foundation.
Enchantment in motion, hope in humanity,
comprehensive division beyond life's fairy tale.

The mist settles, eerily still.
The chamber in living, peaceful pathways, purified
recuperation, rebuilding, re-evaluation?
The observer's dialogue, announcements, visions of
pleasure, spirited elements of desire?
Curiosity, clarity, the weight of past tears, vitality,
the outlet of internal consciousness.
'A sphere of serendipity', transcribed translation, delivered
articulation, soothed, heard.
The passionate dance in a progressive passageway,
in attentiveness to my poetical song.

I greet my inner residents, novel unique arrivals, rest from
timeworn nomadic departures.
Imprinted soulful sharing, a luminescent glow, evolved
advancement, thankfully exuberant.
A connected commonplace, choice, change, chance,
an attentive flicker.

The shining brightness in expressive animated appearance.

The primitive gentle whisperer, delicately humbled in reassurance.
The temperament of nature's language endured survival, the keeper of reality.
My characteristic qualities are saluting glory, a sheltered haven, the oasis in belonging.

Establish stability, far from the remote polluted sea.
Located comfort in a singular compass, an energised procession, guided with nourishment.
In precise possibilities, electric momentum, magical manifestation in dynamic gratification.
Illuminating soothing pacification, perimeters expand in carefully curved contours.
Authentically seen, the key to atmospheric release.
Connected composure, bonded in togetherness, doors ajar, liberating trust.

To walk on uneven cobbled streets, taking my own hand through channelled routes.
I encounter kind-heartedness, riding storms in childlike wildness, my sequential collective.
A traveller reciting intersected worthiness, in endings there are beginnings.

Illustration by Dawn Skelton

The Balancing of Two Sides

E.J

The coastal island of Maryland, a beautiful sight to behold and home to the false creator, a being of absolute power. But this is no home, it is a prison and deep within the island's core, the false creator was trapped, there to be imprisoned, for all its crimes. For the false creator had dared to steal a power that was not theirs to own.

Alpha, Omega; the beginning and the end; the creator and the destroyer, they are in truth two sides to one coin; Beta, the balancer. Alpha was the great creative and Omega was the destroyer, together they could create and demolish anything in seconds. But poor Beta was the balancer between the two sides, as jealousy, inferiority and the longing of acknowledgment grew, tragedy followed. Beta stole Alpha's creation powers for themself, and imprisoned Alpha within the coastal island's core.

The coastal islands, much like the human soul is a beautiful sight to behold. Yet deep within our souls, the two sides of ourselves are imprisoned. Even so, good and bad are two sides to every human. We are simply Beta, the Balancer.

Dodgy Meat
Michael Fairclough

'Badger meat for sale,' the advert said. Impatient, I dialled the number, still cheek to seat in the toilet cubical.

Arranging a meat meeting for that Friday in the pub, he said he'd be in his work uniform so would be clearly visible to passing motorists. The only person there, however, was at first glance lollipop-man and on second my Nana. Approaching her I whispered, 'Nana, what are you doing here?'

'Oh, Norman, it's good to see you.' She started welling up immediately.

'Nana, are you okay?' I questioned, curious as to why she was upset, only for her to reveal my grandad's passing, his side hustle and him wanting to go on his own terms.

'He died the way he lived, stood in the middle of the road waving his lollipop around, only this time he was drunk, naked and in the middle of a motorway. Run over by an ice-cream van, which raises its own questions. I mean what was he doing, selling to hitchhikers? We're having a funeral; well, a cremation. It was a pain be honest, he wanted his ashes spread on the road he worked on, but no matter how much we waved his lollipop, traffic wouldn't stop. As if they knew we were not really lollipop people.'

Then came the Will.

Sat in the living room of my auntie's bungalow, I eyed a selection of my grandad's possessions that were to be divvyed out to the assembled horde, the most eye-catching being his green glass eye in an old jar.

'"And to you, Norman, I leave more than you

bargained for.'"

'What?'

'"And my glass eye. Your Nana wants the jar back, though, and has more details for you when you drop it off."'

At my Nana's house, I knocked on the door only for her to appear from the side gate.

'Ah, Norman, you came. And you brought the jar back! Let me show you around to your grandad's shed, it's where he kept his...'

'Possessions?'

'Shit, most of his shit. Was like a cat, always dragging stuff in. Even used the cat flap once when he lost his keys.'

Inside the shed we were greeted by the usual odds and ends. Old tools, opened tins of paint, a lawn mower unassembled on the table. The biggest thing was a chest freezer next to some strange plants he had on shelves and a coat hook with his work uniform hung up on it as his lollipop leant in the corner. Casually returning grandads eye to one of the shelves in his shed I asked:

'So, is that the meat?'

'Road kill. Waste not want not. He never ate it himself, sold it to mums on the school run. Stopping them crossing the road, like a neon yellow bridge troll. He even crawled out from the manhole cover next to the crossing sometimes, like he was living under there. Had a whole patter: "Road kill, collected by these verry hands. Well, I scrape it up with my lollipop, depends how flat it is. Rat meat, cat meat, bat meat, dog! Ferret meat, pigeon, crow."'

'Hedgehog?' I asked, only to get a rather stern response.

'Never. They're a pain to get the spikes out of. You know, I think he killed some himself, or at least assisted. Don't get me wrong, his lollipop was always bloody from scraping them up, but sometimes it was dented as well. Would take him ages to get it flat again. I think he treated it a bit like a giant tennis racket whenever a bird flew over. He tried to get me to flatten it at first, stuck it in my ironing pile like I wouldn't notice. Ended up having to get a sledgehammer. Was cheaper than buying a replacement and sharpening it... Sorry, I'm rambling again what was I saying?'

'About the road kill?'

'Yeah, that's right, it's all labelled. Not sure you want to keep any. But summer's coming and the rats' tails harden so you could pretend they're a bit like a popsicle stick and lick the hairy bit. He had a few rats in the end. The bats never sold well either after the whole co...'

'Covi—'

'Co-Co Pops Controversy. It was like the horsemeat all over again. I mean, how'd you feel going to buy monkey flavoured cereal, only to find it tasted vaguely chocolaty and contained traces of bat meat? Bloody false advertising! Anyhow, love, your grandad said you can take anything from the shed that takes your fancy, apart from the cut-out of Titchmarsh, he's mine... Oh, and he left a tape in the telly, for your eyes only! Hope it's not porn again. *You've Been Framed* weren't pleased with him for that. Someone still sent us £100 pounds though, so makes you wonder what they did with it,' Nana said before leaving and slamming the door behind her, causing Grandad's eye to turn and look at me from the shelf. Eventually, though, curiosity got the better of me, so after turning Alan and my grandad's eye around I pressed play on the remote.

'Norman! Did I pick Norman?'

'Yes, Hun, you did.' My Nana said from off screen.

'So, I'm dead!' Pressing fast forward I skipped ahead to get to the point of the secret tape.

'Big orange balls, squish you flat if you're not careful or if you annoy the French.'

'What?' I mouthed and rewound again.

'Lollipop men are so much more than you realise.' Finding a starting point of sorts, I let the tape play.

'So, what I'm asking is, will you take up the mantle and become my successor? I know it may not seem like a big deal now. But trust me when I say the job entails more than you can imagine.'

'So, what is it you want me to do?' I asked the tape.

'Pauline, leave the shed.' He said then on the sound of a door shutting continued.

'I'm dying and I need someone to take my place. I thought I had time to find an apprentice but not anymore. Really, I should have left the position to your dad but he's dead to me since he became a jockey. Always looking down at us from his high horse. I was going to make a start next month, actually, but you know. So, I figured why not you? Now, I know this was the last thing you were expecting, so that's why I slapped together this training video. It should tell you everything you need to know and if you still have questions, you can ask one of the others.'

'One of the others? It's not like I know any. Hell, I've never seen more than one lollipop person at a time in my life,' I said to myself aloud. Only for him to reply:

'That's not a problem. We have a directory. You can look us up by area, there's a copy there on the shelf behind you.' He said, pointing from the screen to a book with yellow pages.

'I'm on page 86 but best not look: it's the swimsuit edition,' he said with a wink. Distracted by the stupidness of the comment, I stared at the thick tome only to be pulled back to the screen with his next remark.

'Do you like gardening?'

Confused by the tangent, I looked at the weird plants anew. Almost alien and like nothing I had ever seen, and they seemed to be growing fruit, as orange balls hung from each of the stems - yet appeared too hard to ever be edible.

Grabbing one of the potted plants from the shelf, Grandad sat it down on the table and pushed the tools and debris to the side, to the places they are now since he died.

'Lollipop men don't just guard roads, we guard these,' he said holding up one of the strange plant's orbs.

'This is a hedgehog plant.'

Going over to the plants on the shelves, I examined them closer as my grandad narrated.

'About the size of a tennis ball and sticky to the touch. Just like my prostate, its outer layer will steal your fingerprints if you handle them for too long. Like a Venus flytrap, it catches insects for their nutrients. Gradually dissolving them to be absorbed by the embryo inside.' Turning one in my hand, it caught the light, revealing something - but a plant growing a creature?

'You see, being a lollipop man is a lot like being a nanny or a farmer. Caring for the livestock until they are ready for harvesting.'

'The hedgehogs?'

'No, don't be stupid, the children!' he said, angry at the implication he would ever harm a hedgehog and again, predicting my words.

'Look I'm going to level with you. You don't know anything and that's okay.'

'Thank you?'

'But being a lollipop person is a long and sordid tradition, a birth right, and it's also a bit like a cult to be honest, but you shouldn't hold that against us.'

'You know, you're really not selling me on this,' I said, just eager to leave at this point. And that's when he started to dump lore.

'In the beginning the men of the woods fought the Emerald Man for…'

'Oh, for goodness's sake, fast forward,' I said, aghast

and the dramatics, before pressing the button repeatedly, catching snippets of the bigger picture.

'Rocks of the earth itself...'

'Passed down for generations from…'

'When one of us gets drunk in the pub or as a bedtime…' and lastly, 'Some of us raise Zebras...' Regaining interest, I let him continue.

'To ride into battle when the Emerald man is reborn.'

'Oh, that's fine then.'

'I'm going to miss that part now. Shame really, I was going to name mine The Striped Menace. You should probably get thinking about a name too, it's first come first served like with actors and racehorses.' He sounded sad at the loss of his future zebra. 'Erm what else? Oh, we have a lot of secret meetings. No need to bring a pen and paper, we have someone send out an email with key points after. You will need the uniform and your staff though, and maybe a wild hedgehog as a show of faith. You can have my old one if you like. I call him Mustard.'

'Right.'

'The only other thing I can think of is the sacrifices. You're usually not an active participant unless it's your birthday. More so they're to help set the mood with chanting and the like, a bit like a football game. But the injuries are real.'

At that, my Nana barged back in.

'Oh, before I forget, we had some overspill of road kill into the kitchen fridge. Truth be told, I was trying to sell it at the pub when you walked in, and it completely slipped my mind. Frankly, I just want rid at this point, so I was thinking you could take it home for your tea. It's badger, is that okay?' All the while she was talking I tried to hide my glee at finally getting what I wanted. Making my excuses, I said I'd return next weekend to continue sorting things.

Then, pocketing the meat, I ran home like Charlie with my furry ticket.

Back home I locked the door and closed the curtains. Then set about cooking the badger. Setting the table for my meal I even lit some candles before sitting down to eat. To be candid, it left me in the bathroom all night and made me regret ever ringing that number from the toilet stall. But if nothing else, I had crossed another animal off my list of 101 Exotic Meats to try before you die. Then again, it was not really that exotic, but I suppose it's a bit like house hunting. Location, location and is it mouldy.

Illustration by Michael Fairclough

Lovers and York
John F Goodfellow

(Spring)

I'm in love with both
Her heaven scent
On the streets, redhead, tall and proud.
Hail out of clear blue sky
A rainbow in her right eye, emerald green her left;
Ghosted in this city of ghosts
Sheep on the moors above
The Roman city of my rebirth.
Others, yes, but none so fine, so finite
Driftwood and dry, I, far from my ocean home.
Aquarian and blue-eyed, I miss the scotch mist
      And her laugh, her love strong by breaking
      And remoulding in our own images, hours to
      Know each other, to find love on the west coast.
Who loves me now?

(Summer)

Staring at the ceiling
All work done
Money and bodies spent
We gather our clothes
And head out between city walls
Like elder children
With care, yet careless,
Invincible.

Rusty Rails
Kevin Keld

'Parallel lines appear to meet,' was what my dear, dotty and dishevelled old art teacher used to profess to me as a distinctly uninterested eight-year-old. The catchy phrase entered one ear, skulked around uncomfortably, shrugged its hypothetical shoulders then left as quickly as it arrived. In a desperate attempt to prove him wrong I hatched my plan. It would appear that on every occasion that my poor Aunt Wendy decided to take me on one of her marathon, dreary walks into the countryside, I would stand in the centre of the level crossing down Barmby road. Our eyes would meet and, in that split second, she knew deep down what was coming next. With amazing regularity I would sprint off along the rusty and now defunct railway lines with a burst of energy usually reserved for superheroes. The sight of my aunt in full chase mode, sprinting along the lines complete with lunch bags and thermos flasks swinging around her shoulders, her face a glowing red with either rage or too much exertion must have brought a smile to the faces of whoever was in the railway cottage garden at the time. On the plus side, we could be quite certain that we would not be mown down by a steam engine the size of France. Unfortunately that disagreeable Dr Beeching had waved his magic wand and put paid to any kind of rail travel on that particular line. Aside from trying to nail down the final meeting point of the parallel lines to prove the art teacher wrong, there was another motive for my escape from the clutches of Aunty Wendy. Dr Who was in its heyday, it was the 'go to' sci fi programme for all of us grubby little kids, well it was the *only* sci fi programme for us grubby little kids. The Daleks were my obsession, and I was totally convinced that the accumulated detritus alongside the railway lines actually belonged to a troop of Daleks that used to live in that wooden hut half a mile along the track. Just think how I could impress my school chums if I were to arrive at school clutching the internal workings of a real Dalek.

My obsession with railways continued up to the present day, though I fear that running along the lines these days would just not have the same attraction that it does to a young boy (oh, and of course I am quite unable to make my body move at anything other than walking pace).

On another occasion a school chum (who was in the very enviable position of living in a railway crossing cottage) invited me up for tea. We wasted no time in commandeering the push pull trolley that was in the sidings and gleefully heading off to York railway station in search of adventures. Needless to say, the journey was cut drastically short after only half hour when we realised it would be midnight at this rate before we got anywhere near York.

True Crime
Helen Kenwright

The modern world is full of crimes:
Being wrong on the internet
Wearing the wrong clothes
Having the wrong hair, nails, bag, earrings
Liking the old things
Hating the new things
Being white, black, brown
Being male, female, neither, both -
Somewhere, there is an Ideal,
A being who dodges
all these barriers with the deft body
flicks of an Olympic gymnast.
Never seen, always imagined.

It's a crime
that we can't be comfortable in our own bodies
our own beings,
our own way of doing things.
Be Original, they say, but also Be The Same.
Confusion paralyses us.
The pressure weighs down
As we all remain
        repentant, irredeemable
Criminals.

Grandma, Smoothy Chops and The Candle Fire
Esther Clare Griffiths

(Memoir Extract)

I was on the cusp of starting secondary school - the crowded comprehensive, just a fragmented rumour, full of future promise and pure dread. For the first time, I had my own room. Our tiny attic had been plastered and painted, and for the next eight years I slept on a mattress on the floor, beams in stripes above me mapping out a lonely line. I missed my brother so much, it hurt. I missed my old child-like self. The scratch of records hitting the swirling turntable and music soaring above the rafters, shielded my sadness and granted an escape, a way to tap into and mirror my feelings. The Beatles' *White Album* and A-ha's *Hunting High and Low* reverberated round my sky-blue sloping walls. Later, I would smoke cigarettes out of the skylight, singing Simon and Garfunkel's *'I am A Rock,'* at the top of my voice, edged with irony and laughter.

I had a spare mattress, and friends would stay over, glimpsing a brief window into an eccentric lifestyle. My parents were committed campaigners for peace, and our two-up two-down terrace was often full of left-wing activists, plotting the downfall of the Tories and the end of nuclear weapons. My friends only saw the huge batik peace symbol, its edges covered in protest badges, and the vivid paintwork that gave each room a vastly contrasting colour in thick gloopy gloss. A poster in our narrow hallway with an image of a nuclear mushroom cloud read, *'Home Improvements – Why Bother?'* Our sofas were simply mattresses piled up in an L-shape and our tiny TV was hidden away in my brother's room – rather than a feature of the living room, like all my school friends.

A wooden ladder led up to my bedroom in the sky – an ice box in winter and a sauna in summer. My friends and I climbed up from the vivid, lush-green picture rails and ruby-red painted stairs to crawl across the rafters into parallel mattresses. A navy curtain with pearl-white ribbon edges, hid my clothes and schoolbooks, while the only place we could stand was in the central apex. Alongside the cast iron pan to close my trap door, Dad – tied a thick blue rope to a metal bracket on the beam beneath my window. If there was a fire, I would simply hang onto the rope and climb out my tiny window, cling to the chimney pot and wait for help!

Thankfully I never had to clamber out the window and wait to be rescued from the steep and slippery roof tiles, but we did have a fire. The winter before I turned seventeen, my grandma came to stay alone. Grandpa was operating on patients in a hospital in South America, his hand just as steady deep into retirement as when he was a junior doctor. (He and Grandma spent 30 years in India working for the Salvation Army - he made skin grafts for the poorest, suffering from leprosy, outcast by the caste system, while she was his constant support - admin and much more.) Grandma arrived for her first visit without him, always a matching mauve or beige skirt and jacket set - a contrast to Mum's tie-dye baggy trousers and bright mango-orange henna perm with copper highlights. (Again, my brother and I always called our mum, Fleur - or Mops in jest!) We turned our living room into her bedroom so she didn't have to climb the stairs. On her first night, we tried to reach a lamp to her bed but couldn't find an extension lead. Fleur worried the trailing wires over the floor might trip her over, so fetched a large candle with an electric lighter. Grandma was an insomniac, often reading in chunks through the night, dozing lightly till morning. I didn't see candles as a dangerous fire hazard – sure, we burnt them every evening for dinner, their flames flickering over the walls and lighting up the peace batik for hours afterwards. My grandma must have drifted off to sleep while the candle slipped down the side of her mattress, smouldering silently for hours. I awoke in the dead of night to sounds of a strangulated 'Help!' Rushing downstairs, the flames were as high as the ceiling, the room crammed with thick black smoke. Fleur comforted her mum while my brother, Pops and I dashed to the bathroom, soaked towels in water and hurled them onto the fire, causing great hissing sounds, like a myriad of snakes. We all ran to the bathroom, soaked towels in water and hurled them onto the fire, causing great hissing sounds, like a myriad of snakes. Even blacker wet smoke swirled over my head, but by the time the fire brigade arrived, there was just a smattering of glinting embers. Grandma climbed into the ambulance with Fleur, pale and quiet. She was in shock - though once she reached the comforting bright hospital lights, she was able to make jokes about being a retired arsonist. Pops refused to go with her in the ambulance, though I tried hard to persuade him as he leaned against the blackened wall, his breath laced with course, asthmatic wheezes. He was wheezy for weeks afterwards.

Most of our games and puzzles were lost in the fire. Stored under the mattresses in wide wooden drawers, just a few charred tin soldiers and chips of puzzle pieces gave any clue of our childhood toys. Pops' two antique oil paintings – a drummer boy and an aristocrat, gifted from his grandfather, were burnt right through, the remnants coated in thick, clammy soot. I had watched the little drummer boy playing a wooden flute throughout my childhood, often wondering why his eyes were so sad. He appeared on all our walls and made all the moves with us - from Ballygelly and Belfast, to Gateshead and Durham. The other painting was of a Renaissance man, in cavalier frilly cuffs, long brown hair curling on his shoulders, his thoughtful eyes following me around the room wherever I went. We fondly referred to him as *'Smoothy Chops.'* Dad took him down from above the mantlepiece and leant him against the wall upstairs, leaving a large white imprint in the blackened walls.

One afternoon after school, my brother and I were watching *Neighbours* when he stepped back without looking and put his foot through the painting. A long tear, just missing Smoothy Chops' well-oiled face ran through the deep mahogany background, a seam of frayed cream, ragged at the edges. In a cruel twist, the paintings were to be valued and insured a couple of days afterwards. They were far and away the most valuable possessions in our entire house. We cleaned black smoke from white walls, piling up a mass of sooty rags that lay heaped by the fireplace for weeks. The painting of the little drummer boy was so badly burnt, Pops couldn't bear to see his charred demise, and rushed straight into our back lane, swiftly chucking the blackened, once golden frame into our scruffy, grey wheely bin. Later, after tea, I ventured outside to empty some leftovers and caught sight of the drummer boy's melancholy eyes staring out bleakly amongst a sea of potato peelings and scraps.. Once, I emptied some leftovers outside and caught sight of his melancholy eyes staring out bleakly amongst a sea of potato peelings and scraps. *Smoothy Chops* was cleaned and hung back above the mantlepiece, still noble, but uninsured and worthless.

As far as I know, Grandma kept quiet about the fire, never

breathing a word to Grandpa. He remained blissfully unaware for the rest of his days. I do recall Pops cursing his mother-in-law, muttering *that bloody woman* under his breath as he tried to plaster over the charcoaled walls.

Three Poems
Paul Francisco

elsewhere

sleepy bumblebee
        light aircraft drones …   in summer blue
                waves of distant radio
      mow the lawn
and thaw the glassy icecubes…

and we still need
 to escape
     through the leafy gateway
 of a book
       to less…   *suburban* realms
                where we can fly

       undeadened
       by heat
       and languidity….

in our dreams   we are
                sleeping no more

electric ant

hold a tiny stinging ant
in the closed palm
of your hand
and feel
it trying to sting
its way out
of your grasp

it's persistent, I'll give it that…

after half-an-hour, however,
it falls quiet
and stops stinging

do you feel calmer?

blossom

My heart is a tender bird
held in a cage of bones.
Tears fall when the cold returns,
wet cherry blossom
scattered on pavements.

I sat on the bench
and gazed upon the pavement café
beneath a blossom canopy
and heard the fiddler play
his melancholy air

My heart is a tender bird
held in a cage of bones…

and as the clouds parted
briefly I could feel
the warm spring sunshine
upon my uncovered head
then a gentle smattering
of applause
broke
as his music
drew
to its close.

The Cheque's in the Post.
Nic Campbell

My first day back through the hospice doors. Fear and dread, yet a place of peace and hope. I signed myself in, name, who I'm visiting, car reg and the time.

The feeling of familiarity came flooding back. My favourite receptionist saw my stance and the warm volunteer, she took my hand. They saved me from falling when Mum was dying, my first port of call, they chatted and chatted, so I didn't fall.

Through the door came my counsellor with a smile and calm voice, a seat and introduction, giving me time. Then I was off! Talk, talk, talk for an hour (that was I not her). How did she do it, how did she hear my pain and my fear?

What made me think I was here to tidy up my loose ends, sort my emotions, or even make amends? I thought I would sit and cry, but I didn't, I was numb, just numb at it all. You let me talk and then talk until slowly the lid it popped off.

I wasn't knocked back and I wasn't knocked down this time and told it was rubbish, I'm rubbish, I'm not good enough. You heard me, you held me in this quiet calm space, you validated me as a human being in my own right. I felt crazy, felt guilt and felt shame for feeling the anger, the swearing it came.

The huge gap in my life gave me time to think, I felt free and felt shit for daring to be. But you listened and listened and helped me some more, took hold of my pain and somehow contained it. Oh the memories, *FUCK OFF* I shouted. I never felt judged, just held with a sensitivity that only you could give me.

I couldn't help but tell you how brilliant you are,

shouted from the rooftops, the whole of St. Gemma's know about this counsellor who quietly listens. 'The cheque's in the post,' you said. I laughed out loud and you laughed with me. I think you were proud?

That week the CEO at reception listened to my rambling of respect for St. Gemma's and I could not stop. 'I need you to know, my counsellor here is next to none, she's amazing,' I said. Then when I told you 'I've been singing your praises,' I heard it again; 'The cheque's in the post,' and we laughed some more.

You helped me to laugh, you helped me to cry to look at my confusion and chaos until exhaustion crept in. Then gently you let me go into the world outside. I took all my new learning and healing to join my new tribe.

The Morning Light
Enoch McFadden

Morning light comes early here,
solstice not long past.
Fetching in a cold new year;
sparkling dewy grass.

Winter gulps down morning light,
its cruel hands eclipse
blood-dyed sun of summer night
that warms our evening bliss.

Dawn solitude becomes a stack
of ashy loneliness.
The quiet hours, world asleep,
now fog and icy darkness.

Come, come, winter solstice,
the enduring of the day.
Bring morning light and time for
imagination's play.

Arteries of frost still lie
across the winter ground.
Ever early dawn rays shine
on new life all around

the wooded glades, wild riverbanks
and mystic forest lands.
Morning light rejuvenates
all life in marshy sands.

Days go by and light is now
around us when we rise.
Weeks pass weeks and morning light
brings beauty to our eyes.

Morning light is harbinger
for sonic revelry.
Drone and dirge fade away for
trumpet and bouzouki

ringing out on red-sun nights
through wet and humid air.
Respite taken from tall glasses,
beads condense: smudged with care.

Evening sun on bodies wet
with sweat from long days' bathing
in the solar showers sent
hot with solstice turning.

More light! More light! Time stretches long
for daydreams, love, and joyful song.
For glances shared and secrets bared,
for wine and laughter overheard.

Bare feet across cool, dry grass.
Books read in open air.
The hum of life in all we pass;
Oh, morning light. Stay here.

Bloodstained-glass
Minnie Lansell

The cold metal toy soldiers pressed into Jasper's palms. He stared at the other soldiers stood neatly in a well-worn sweet tin bearing the name Eric. His heart wilted at the thought of his dad. In a time when almost everything was unfamiliar, these precious treasures felt like home. Elodie had pretty much stayed in her room since they had lived with Miriam and he had followed suit. It wasn't that he disliked his Great-Aunt, he just didn't know her.

He stretched out on his back and looked at the ceiling. The paint was flaking off. This was the theme of the entire house. Damp, dirty, old and forgotten. Their modern furniture intruded against the backdrop of fusty white sheets shrouding archaic furnishings. He watched the light dance on the wall for a moment, appreciating the beauty of it. He had chosen this room because of the stained-glass window. An elaborate yellow sun on a blue background. El had one too. Hers was a crow sitting in a beautiful tree.

A bell rang. They had noticed upon arrival yesterday that the house had service bells which still worked. He checked his watch; 1pm, lunch time. Miriam had spent most of the previous day setting up their bedrooms and the kitchen. Each of them had given the others space; since their mum died, Miriam had lost her old life as much as they had.

The kitchen was on the ground floor, but slightly lower, down a few stone steps at the rear of the house. It had a large 19th century cast iron range oven and a huge wooden table in the middle. The window furthest to the left was dark under the curtain of ivy outside. Miriam was talking to a man sitting at the table. He was a slender build, bald on top with whitened hair around his ears. His glasses were thick-rimmed and he wore a checked shirt under his dungarees.

'This is Barnaby Paul. He's the gardener and caretaker,' said Aunt Miriam. 'This is Jasper,' she said, gesturing towards him, 'and this is Elodie coming now.'

Elodie entered the kitchen clutching a book close to her chest. Sadness seemed to suck the colour from her usually bright blue eyes.

'Hello. Call me Barny. I'm the gardener. Welcome to Spiorad House. It's nice to meet ya both. How ya settlin' in?'

Elodie shrugged and started hard at the wall. Jasper could see her eyes starting to tear up. 'Hi,' he said. 'How did you say the name again?'

'Spiorad,' said Barny. 'Spy-rad'.

The room fell silent. Nobody seemed to know what to say now.

'I'm sorry it's sandwiches again,' said Miriam. 'The electricity was switched on this morning, but this stove is gas and that's not been uncapped yet. Maybe we could order take away for dinner?' She looked towards Jasper but nodded towards Elodie.

'Yeah, whatever,' said Elodie still avoiding all eye contact. 'Don't care. Do what you want.' Her eyes glazed deeply and then tears cascaded down her face. Miriam reached her hands towards Els but she turned away.

'Now it might be outa turn, what me bein' the outsider an' all,' said Barny, 'an' I know you've been through more than most kids yer age. And it seems to me that all three of you have lost a lot, but do ya know what you've gained?'

Elodie frowned at him.

'Each other,' he said simply. 'As hard as it gets, young miss, you've a brother and an Auntie standin' right by yer side.'

There was another silence. Miriam held out her arms and Elodie nodded. They both cried. Jasper glanced around the room for something to focus on before he started too. Barny smiled and pushed a plate towards him. Jasper began to demolish the sandwich. 'Now then young miss, Miss Emmett mentioned you like to draw, is that right?'

Elodie nodded.

'Oh, please call me Miriam,' said Aunt Miriam.

'Well then, I've got some weedin' to do. How'd ya fancy sketchin some flowers an' keepin' me company?'

Elodie nodded again. Barny handed Miriam a handkerchief, winked at her and led Elodie back into the main house collecting her sandwich as he went.

Aunt Miriam stood with her back to Jasper wiping her eyes on the hanky.

'It's really hard,' he said. 'She's struggling.' His eyes unfocussed briefly as a montage of painful events flashed across his mind on fast forward. 'Thanks for not letting them… split us up.' He gave a weak smile. Aunt Miriam walked over to him, tilted his face up to hers and wiped peanut butter off his chin.

'Thank you,' she said. She crushed him in a momentary embrace. 'Now I'm all for grieving and what not, but enough for today. Elodie is occupied so why don't you go and explore! We've no idea what secrets this house is keeping.' She put on a smile. 'I expect a full report at dinner!'

The house was dank and smelled fusty and old. The foyer was lit by large grimy windows on the front of the house. Properly looking at it for the first time, Jasper was reminded of the film Beauty and the Beast. The stairs swept upwards to the landing where the house split left and right. The kitchen was down a few steps to the right behind the stairs, along with other utility areas and a cold stone stairway that led down to a room with many rotted shelves and ceramic jars. Apparently, this was a buttery; where foods were stored before fridges were invented. Jasper had already gone right, to the east end of the house, where the grand banqueting room and boot room were. Right at the far eastern point was a wooden arched door. This opened into a small stone chapel with an altar and wooden pews. It had a bright stained-glass window of a rose and rain drops. The sunlight had painted the image onto the stone floor.

He headed left this time, past the staircase to a pair of large double doors. Inside was a room with a massive fireplace and heavy moth infested drapes at the windows. There were large paintings on the walls. Many looked like Lords and Ladies. This had to be the drawing room. Through a far door Jasper found himself in a corridor which, to the right led back to the foyer and left, to a study with leather chairs, a large desk and cabinets full of trinkets. Beyond that was a school room, some sort of servants dining room and finally, at the far west end of the house Jasper stood in amazement. Shelves upon shelves of books. Big, wingback leather chairs and a fireplace. The bookcases were so tall they had ladders and above them the front half of the room opened out into the first floor! He smiled as his heart lightened. El loved nothing more than to lose herself in a good book. Hopefully it would lift her spirits a little.

There was a spiral staircase leading up to the first floor. Jasper investigated and found himself in the upper level of the library, though smaller than below, it was impressive to look over the walkway which ran around the exterior. As he was taking it all in, he noticed splashes of coloured light on the floor. It was another stained-glass window. Most of the light was blocked by the ivy, but he could just make out a horse and something long, like a lance, maybe? Could it be a knight?

Most of the rooms on the first floor were bedrooms. Three of which had stained-glass windows. The last room before the landing and stairs was a nursery. Victorian looking toys and a pram sat preserved under more than a century worth of dust. The windows in here were different to any he had seen. Instead of one big stained-glass window there were twelve smaller ones.

As he ascended a crooked wooden staircase to the attic, he noticed how simple and worn everything was. The servants' quarters consisted of eight small rooms with beds and chamber pots. What seemed out of place were the stained-glass windows. Only five rooms had them. Two were darkened by ivy, though they had spots of light sneaking through. Two more were darkened, though this seemed quite strange to Jasper as there was no ivy on the other side of the window. Sunlight came through the clear glass, but not the coloured pictures. The eighth room contained a window depicting purple flowers and a green background. The rest of the attic was storage. Jasper had fun rummaging through things. He figured there was stuff from the last five centuries or more. Wearing a big maroon hat with a moulted feather in it and carrying a metal fencing sword he headed downstairs, eventually announcing his presence in the kitchen by challenging Aunt Miriam to a duel!

After dinner Elodie was still very sad but seemed more accepting of the situation after an afternoon of peaceful drawing.

As soon as the dishes were done, Jasper dragged Elodie down the west corridor. 'Now close your eyes. It's a surprise!'

El raised an eyebrow momentarily, but then agreed to indulge him and closed her eyes. Jasper opened the double doors and led her inside. 'Don't peek, I've got you,' he said, leading her to the middle of the room where the ceiling disappeared into the upper story. 'Ready. Three, two, one!'

Elodie opened her eyes. As she took it all in her mouth hung open and her eyes brightened. Jasper slipped his hand into hers and pulled her to the spiral staircase. Elodie walked around and around, running her fingers across the treasure trove of books.

'Aunt Miriam and Barny were talking about tackling the ivy,' she told him. 'Apparently, it's been like this for decades. Barny said a guy was here about six years ago but left without saying! And the family before that didn't stick around long either. He said he was told the last family to actually live here left in the 1700's after a tragedy. I don't know what happened though. He went quiet and then started talking about weeds.' She looked solemnly at her brother. 'It's so hard. I want to be excited about this,' she waved her hand around her, 'but I feel guilty every time I smile. Like being happy means I don't care about Mum.' She took a deep, shaky breath and continued. 'I do care. I miss her so much. And Dad. I'm sorry if I'm being hard to handle. I'm here for you, you know that right? Jazzy?'. Her smile seemed to grow out of happy memories flashing behind her eyes.

Jasper nodded. 'I know. And I know about feeling guilty. For smiling. For liking Aunt Miriam. For just being a kid, I guess.'

They hugged. Elodie buried her face into his shoulder and let out a deep sigh. She slipped her hand into his and they headed back along the first-floor corridor to the top of the stairs.

'And there are actually quite a lot of stained-glass windows, even in the attic!' he was saying. Elodie frowned.

'Isn't the attic the servants' quarters?' she asked.

He nodded 'I think so.'

Jasper stopped. Elodie's tablet was charging on the landing. He bent down to unplug it for her. The socket dislodged in his hand. There was a loud fizzing noise and his whole body instantly felt like it had nettle stings, even inside. As Jasper hit the floor, Elodie screamed and screamed.

Jasper noticed how shadowy the landing had become.

His attention was quickly drawn to a stained-glass window, though he didn't recall it being there before. A dove shone from it, enticing him to look through. As he pressed his face to the glass, his body chilled. On the other side was the landing, Aunt Miriam had her arm around a distraught Elodie, and Barny was doing CPR on Jasper's own, lifeless body.

Till Dance, do us part
G.V. Terolli

Clement and a distant shift in the sky's color
Create a soft backdrop of warm colors.
A slight sense of the warmth of the sun rising with a grin.

His hand touches mine.
Our steps cross each other as our eyes meet,
There is a shine to his face, a glow perhaps.

The music is smooth and precise, and
A mixture of laughter amidst the instruments.
Exhaustion, fatigue fills me, but as a distant memory.

We waltz together in this flow of time,
Speaking a secret language.
Our synced, rhythmic heartbeat.

Dance, till do us part.

The Tale of the Disappearing Coat
Lee King

Back in 1982, when I was an 11-year-old with a keen sense of fashion (or at least I thought so), my mum bought me a coat that I absolutely despised. It was brown, padded, and made of corduroy – everything that a cool kid's coat shouldn't be. At the time, the must-have item was a sleek, black Harrington jacket, the epitome of coolness in my school. Unfortunately, my new coat was the exact opposite, and I dreaded the thought of being seen in it.

Shortly after acquiring this monstrosity of a coat, my class went on a week-long school trip to Bewerley Park, the outdoor activity centre. This was my chance! I devised a cunning plan to "lose" the coat and hopefully convince my mum to get me the Harrington I so desperately wanted.

As the trip came to an end, I left the coat behind, confident in my plan. I returned home, coatless but hopeful. My mum, of course, was furious. 'Where's your coat?' she demanded. I put on my best innocent face and said, 'I lost it. It's gone forever.'

For a brief moment, I thought I had succeeded. Little did I know, the universe had other plans. The following week, another class from my school visited the same outdoor centre. To my horror, the teachers had found my coat. My mum, ever the vigilant parent, had written my name on the label, ensuring it would find its way back to me.

The coat was returned to the school and handed back to me in front of my amused classmates. I couldn't believe my misfortune. But I wasn't ready to give up yet. Determined to rid myself of the hideous coat once and for all, I hatched a new plan.

At the end of the school field was a patch of waste ground, the school was called Westfield Junior School and we called the waste ground weggie mud hills, as it had piles of earth pushed in to little hills, a beck ran along the side of said hills and the school field, some playtimes we would dare each other to jump over the beck, many a shoe, trainer and welly was lost in the becks thick sticky mud, resulting in forlorn children hopping back to afternoon lessons in only one shoe, but that is a different story!

There was also a pond which was full of newts and frogs, but best of all a big muddy bog, I made a detour to the bog with a stick in hand, I pushed the coat deep into the mud, watching with satisfaction as it disappeared from sight. Finally, I was free.

When I got home, I put on my best sad face and told my mum the tragic news: I had lost the coat again. This time, it was truly gone. My mum, perhaps sensing the futility of the situation, eventually relented and got me the black Harrington jacket I had wanted all along.

Looking back, it's a wonder the lengths I went to just for a coat. But fashion was a serious business for an 11-year-old in 1982!

New Book
Sue Leung

He had chosen his seat well: halfway back, on the right, with an unrestricted view. There was no dropped gum to permanently weld his shoes to the floor. On catching his reflection in the bus window, John smoothed his hair. He sighed, opened his book and smelt the newness. The bus had left urban tarmac, which was replaced by blackthorn. Savage thorns hiding behind dainty blossom. Leaves yet to unfurl. He swapped sunglasses for his prescription pair and snapped the case shut.

Leaning back, John smiled and started to read.

Lightning Star Scene
James Wilson

Somewhere in the Sky between the stars and planets was a space colony. There lived Astrid and Erold: Astrid was a scientist, Erold an engineer who kept the space fleet in the air. Astrid and Erold were soon to be taking a mission to Sapris, a rival colony. What lay in store for them they did not know: the Sapris colony had a reputation of danger. The only backup Astrid and Erold had was a communication link with base down below the star studded sky.

Can they save their colony?

The year was 2056 and they had on the colony two types of vehicle: giant aluminium encased space trucks, and two bigger ships with giant encased viewing platforms and an oval covering which allowed those inside to exist in space. The ships were giant, very high tech with advanced technology.

The day came when Erold would take one of the ships on an expedition in space to pick up a newcomer on another vessel in space. This ship was a steel silver with red stripes and had high tech lit cockpit which had purple and indigo lights.

The newcomer, Lebana, was trained in tele-communications for space, a scientist a bit younger than Erold and Astrid. It was her first visit to the colony: she had trained in the USA at a space centre there. She was. a medic, too, and Erold knew they needed her at the colony, and she was bringing much-needed supplies.

Erold boarded his ship and took his seat under the controls in the cockpit. He pressed the ignition and the dashboard lit up with a mix of white and orange buttons. There were switches and a throttle and controls for guiding the ship inside the cockpit.

The engines started and there was an ear-piercing roar from the engines causing turbulence in the ship. The noise was phenomenal. He was on his way.

His ship cruised through the bright glistening stars, but their ship was not performing well. Erold tried levelling the controls but there was a loud bang, and the ship shook. Erold set the controls to cruise control on autopilot. He glanced out of the cockpit window, and one of the booster engines was on fire. He quickly put his helmet and space suit on. Erold's body felt compressed in the space suit. He let out a gasp before the first supply oxygen came through his lungs felt tight and his chest felt strained. He had a small extinguisher and a link from the ship to the booster engine so he would be able to get back to the ship. Erold's only hope was to extinguish the fire.

He opened the cargo hold, grasping the extinguisher. The line he had attached to a belt on his waist slowly extended as he trod on the wing of the ship to reach the booster engine.

The flames from the fire were rising, the smoke was circulating round him. He was glad of the oxygen that came through his helmet. The heat from the blaze was immense and the flames flickered at his feet.

Erold tried to extinguish the fire and held onto the lead; the flames were flicking up fast as he tried to fight the fire. His lungs tightened; he boosted oxygen to combat the restricted breathing. Finally the power of the extinguisher started to extinguish the flames. The fire was out but there were long stretches of blackened smoke damage.

Erold followed the lead attached to his waist back to the ship, bit by bit. He went on the intercom and explained what had happened to Astrid back at the colony. She reassured Erold that Lebana was on the vessel at the meeting point at the base, waiting for Erold with supplies.

Erold ran the booster engine which had been on fire at a very low rev. Erold was not far from the base where Lebana was. He slowly approached the ship base through the stars and pulled up by Lebana's ship.

She was in full space gear already with her helmet with oxygen. She helped Erold load the supply crates onto the ship, talking to him, a little apprehensive at going to the colony. Erold reassured her and explained it would all be fine, and that Astrid will be there at the colony. He told her about the fire but said it should get them to the colony safely.

Lebana and Erold returned to the ship, with their supplies loaded on, and Erold started the engine. He was confident the ship would make it back to the colony.

Time passed and Erold said to Lebana, 'You can see our colony there, in space under the oval covering.' Erold kept calm but he was losing control of the ship – the fire from the engine had caused a lot of damage. He set the ship's landing code in motion. The ship slowly descended towards the steel platform, but it was like descending into a volcano. There wasn't much air: their oxygen supplies were working hard and each of them were finding it hard to breathe.

Erold said, 'We're not going to be able to land, our oxygen supplies won't last.' He hit an orange circular control. 'I'm getting us out of here.' There was an almighty bang, and the ship shook, sending them crashing out of their seats. The ship filled with smoke.

Erold pulled back on his controls and the engines

created a tremendous roar. They were soon on their climb back up out of there.

They got closer and closer to the colony, then arrived, Erold landing confidently on the landing pad. Erold and Lebana put their space suits on and Erold opened the cargo door.

Astrid was there in full space suit to greet them and from this first meeting Astrid and Lebana chatted and hit it off from the start. Erold unloaded the supplies. He would need to work on that engine that caught fire.

Under the oval covering in their space gear, the three of them sat down to eat and Erold chatted with their new guest. They all had separate quarters to sleep under the oval covering. It had been a long day, so they tried to get some sleep. But Erold knew there would be more to overcome in their colony.

The next day, Erold got up early and put full space gear on. He went to where he'd stored the new supplies. He hadn't heard a ship or vessel in the night, but the supplies were in disarray and quite few missing. They must have been raided by the Sapris colony!

Sapris had a bad reputation. There had been rumours of them being armed. Erold and Astrid had a lockup with some rifles in case they encountered anything out of the ordinary and had been trained to use them in emergencies. They knew that Sapris was supplying stolen goods to the other colonies in the solar system.

Erold decided with Astrid and Lebana that they would take a ship from their colony and try to reason with the crew on Sapris to get their missing supplies back.

Erold set the ship's controls for the short route to the Sapris Colony. It had taken time for Astrid, Erold and Lebana to prepare their ship. They had informed the ground crew of their mission and re-iterated that rifles must remain in the lockup on the ship.

Erold had planned they would depart that evening. He knew the three of them may face many perils on the Sapris colony. Astrid, Erold and Lebana made sure they were in full space gear with oxygen supplies.

They'd boarded the ship and Erold had shut the cargo door. This was it. They were going to Sapris and there was no turning back. Erold knew they faced much danger, but the stolen supplies were crucial if their colony was to survive. They had to retrieve them.

They had also loaded onto the ship a crate containing luxuries: alcohol, tobacco and few items of the best food supplies they had to try and barter with the Sapris colony.

The ship's engines let out huge roar and there was much turbulence. As they cruised through space, the stars glistening, their colony disappeared behind them. Hours went by, each of them strapped into seats inside the ship.

Finally it reached 11:47 pm and they made it to the Sapris Colony.

They went on the satellite intercom and told the Sapris crew they were landing, and the ship began the descent down. It was set up in law that incoming vessels to colonies had to use satellite communication to land. It was like going into a volcano. The ship heated and Erold was sweating - this planet was well above the temperature of their planet colony. Through the ship's viewing platforms he could see it was like burning lava on the planet edge, but there was a steel landing platform. Their ship was conditioned to deal with high temperatures so it should be fine.

The Sapris crew were now visible. Erold could make out gun turrets on platforms – they were all manned.

All the Sapris crew were armed, too. Astrid used the satellite intercom to speak to their home crew. She said,

'We're landing on Sapris. They have gun turrets manned and they are all armed. Send out another ship, we're going to need a backup fleet.'

Erold had set the ship's landing code in motion, and the ship was slowly descending towards the steel platform, but it was like descending into a volcano. There wasn't much air; their oxygen supplies were working hard and each of them were finding it hard to breathe.

'We're not going to be able to land,' Erold said. Our oxygen supplies won't last, we'll perish.' He hit the orange circular control. 'I'm getting us out of here.'

There was another almighty bang.

The ship shook, sending them crashing out of their seats, and the cockpit filled with smoke. Erold pulled back on his controls, and the engines created a tremendous roar. They were on their climb back up out of there.

Then the ship shook again, sending them crashing out of their seats. The smoke was getting thicker.

'They've opened fire from the right gun turret!' Astrid said.

'I can still get us out of here.' Erold hit more buttons and at last the ship was moving fast through space. They had made the climb out of Sapris and they were a good distance now from the gun turrets. They'd made it! Their oxygen supplies were still working hard but the smoke was clearing, and they could breathe. Erold set the repair protocols going and Astrid took a communication from their ground base. They had said they now would send a recovery ship to them, and troops were being sent out to Sapris.

Lebana Astrid and Erold could now see their colony again - safety.

It had been a failed mission but also a successful mission as they were all safe. This wasn't over, though. The intercom from ground base said, 'Our troops landed on Sapris. We have overcome them for now. But the battle is far from over.'

They would return to Sapris with a bigger fleet of ships. They knew the Sapris mercenaries would regroup.

This battle had to be won !

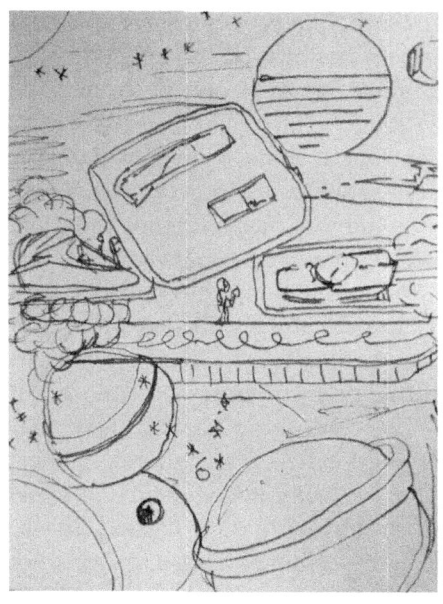

Illustration by James Wilson

The Final Goodbye
Lauran Kay Ransom

Goodbye. One word, seven letters, two syllables. It's such a simple word but a word with the power to break a kingdom, destroy a queen or crack a fragile heart.

When did you last hear it? A real goodbye?

The last time I heard it and it she meant it was my nanna's final goodbye.

She was a strong woman, a woman who would help any and every person she could. A woman who at age 89 was helping people half her age, shopping and gardening. For as long as I could remember she was never ever still - she was always doing something she enjoyed baking, cleaning, gardening; her home always filled with the scents of roses form the snippets she was growing for all her friends.

Do you happen to remember those old washing machines? Hers was grey and looked almost like a spaceship in the kitchen. They sounded like rockets too making every wall vibrate when it spun her favourite dresses, pockets always hiding tissues. The soapy water emptied into your washing up bowl for you to pour into the sink yourself. When we were done, Nanna would relax into her old chair and turn up the fire even if it was already 90 degrees in summer.

At night I would go into my mum's old bedroom, still light outside the shadow of next door's plum tree would be outlines on the pink curtains. It always reminded me of the sharp sweet jam she used to enjoy making. Jar after jar after jar. Then I'd hear her shuffle past to the bathroom, curlers in her hair and teeth long taken out and forgotten about.

When she said her final goodbye, these comforting familiar memories flooded my mind. That final goodbye, the tiny words on dry chapped lips, eyes closing against a long hard happy life.

This goodbye I relive every time I close my eyes. Every hydrangea plant swaying in the breeze, every black jelly baby saved, every Hovis biscuit buttered for breakfast reminds me of that incredible woman.

Whose goodbye is this goodbye for you?

The Holy Trinity
S J L

Foryouforyouforyou

Deep underwater,
The current drags me
Further out to
See something clear,
Down in myself
I'm drowning in my sins,
I'll take shelter
Somewhere quiet,
Somewhere within
Find a temple,
Something my body
Should have been.
Ruins remain,
My soul is stained
I'll turn myself to wine
For him
I'll walk across the water
For you
Drag myself down further
For you
Everything I do, I do it
FOR YOU

Illustration by SJL

I FIND GOD

I FIND GOD
WHEN I LOOK AT YOU
I FIND GOD
IN THE QUIET HOURS
IN BETWEEN
THE MOON AND
THE MORNING DEW
I FIND GOD
EVEN WHEN I DON'T WANT TO

Illustration by SJL

Delectable

I want you to consume me
not like Hannibal
but something soft
something more palatable

with flowers on the table
delicate, decorated, delectable
'everything that lives and moves
will be food for you'
     genesis 9:3

Illustration by SJL

Dancing Mice
Sheryl Cunningham

The rain was beating hard against the roof as the cold air whistled through the station platform.

Midnight approached as I waited for the last train back to Blossom Road.

I sat on the cold metal seat, my mind preoccupied with thoughts of how hard – mentally - this evening has been.

I'd gone to a friend's engagement party alone, surrounded by people without a clue who I was, and vice versa. Which led to strangers being inquisitive; wanting to know, what felt like, my life story. I became a repeating robot; telling the same tale to all who asked, and a fair few did, so now my brain was mentally drained, and I was physically exhausted. All I wanted was the sanctuary of home.

Cold, wet, and miserable, I stared at the old clock hands moving slowly round its face, only another eighteen minutes to wait.

As the last couple of commuters got on their last train to Apple Garth, lights started flickering around me. I, and most of the local residents, were used to only having the bare minimum of lights working or going out. So this evening was no different, or so I thought.

My vision had adjusted to the dimness, and from the corner of my eye I noticed tiny shadows moving back and forth from underneath the maintenance door further down from where I was sitting.

Grateful for the distraction I decided to investigate what was going on.

Turning slowly towards the door, I watched as two little figures came scuttling from behind a bin, then dashed to and fro between the gap beneath the door and a rubbish pile underneath an empty bench; half eaten sandwiches still laying in their packaging, crumbs of what I presumed were once sausage rolls and opened crisp packets laid in the day's dirt like it was a graveyard.

I could hear the delicate rustling of my two new-found friends, rummaging through what looked like an open packet of cheese and onion crisps. I could just make out the colour blue. I'd always thought cheese and onion should have been green.

The squeaks mixed with the drumming of the rain and the ethereal hum of the electricity cables. It made for quite a strange, relaxing kind of rhythm.

The mice stopped and looked around, nervous, as if some predator had come onto the scene. Then the electric humming grew louder, wind howled down the tunnel. Suddenly the harsh glare of engine lights followed by metal carriages clanking on the rails rolled by with such speed. A heavy goods train, probably on its way to Pottermouth power station.

I turned back to see if the mice were as mesmerised as me, but they had scuttled away.

A minute later the last carriage disappeared into the darkness. I noticed my furry friends had come back, and I smiled.

The larger mouse, whom I named Bob, poked his head out from behind a coffee cup, sniffing the air. The other, smaller, one – Chel – busied itself by munching on a tiny piece of sausage roll, looking up every now and then just to make sure it was safe to continue with its feast.

As they were rummaging, Chel uncovered a big chunk of chicken from beneath a sandwich wrapper. Straight away Bob noticed; I liked to believe they would have said, 'Hmmm yummy, I shall make it mine, all mine'. Which reminded me immediately of Gollum from Lord of the

Rings.

I could see that Chel knew that Bob was coming up behind, he could smell him. Turning quickly, and stood up on his back legs, twitching his nose and whiskers, he held tightly to the treasure. Bob continued to approach his 'so called' friend, slowly, deliberately trying to intimidate. This lasted for what felt like minutes, whereas in reality it was merely seconds.

They were now face to face, both on their back legs, poised for the battle to begin, the treasure now on the floor between them.

I held my breath, watching with anticipation, and then it started.

Back and forth they started fighting, turning in circles. The flickering light placed their shadows against the stone wall, making them look like dancers. I started to imagine that I was watching a ballet, honoured with a private show, and I knew exactly which one.

The Nutcracker by Tchaikovsky and *The Dance of the Sugar Plum Fairy*, one of my favourites. With the music playing inside my head and my friends dancing away, I had completely forgotten about my evening. The moment was fleeting but it felt amazing.

As I watched, another little mouse appeared onto the 'stage', sneaking slowly in the shadows towards them, stopping just a little way back from the dancing duo, watching and waiting. Then suddenly it rushed forward, grabbed the treasure, turned and ran towards the maintenance door. The cheeky, clever fellow! I quietly laughed.

By the time Bob and Chel had noticed, the treasure and the other mouse had gone, and so my private performance had ended.

Knowing there was nothing to be done and probably exhausted, they went back to slowly rummaging through the graveyard of waste, disappointed, yet hopefully friends again.

I went back to listening to the drumming of rain while waiting for my train, though now I had a smile upon my face, warmth in my heart and I felt less stressed.

I have never forgotten about Bob and Chel; every time I wait for a train, I always keep an eye out for my dancing friends, and a few scraps of food.

Poems
Angela Bridge

Two Poems After 'This is Just to Say' by William Carlos Williams

1. This is Just to Say

>Just to let you know
>nicked the beer
>U had in the fridge
>U was probably
>saving 4 2nite
>Soz
>got carried away
>N drank the lot.

2. This is Just to Say

>Just to let you know
>I haven't forgotten
>the cornflakes.
>Hot milk turned cold
>you left on the table
>in a Peter Rabbit bowl
>for me when I got home
>from school.
>You said I had to eat them all
>even though the globs
>of milk made me sick.

Inspirational Woman

When she let go of her mother's skirt
she toddled off in high heels
her aunt had left in the hall
listing, like a drunk
careful not to fall.

Glued to the beauty tips in My Guy
she read at the kitchen table
curating the perfect bow of the lips
to take shots at New Romantic older boys
with just the right amount of wild.

Her wedding dress was as off-white
as her mother's face
at the sight of the tiny spot
of blood-stained lace veiling
her gaze as she inched down the aisle.

She could paint over the blackest eye,
and with a smudge of careful application
concealed hairline scars to the left side
of her upper lip, hermetically sealing
her long lost smiles.

She pivoted on the deadliest thread
of woven silky lies she trampled
in high heeled Jimmy Choo shoes
but didn't falter once with heavy bags
the day she turned and walked away.

And, still, she did not fall.

Acknowledgements

Thank you to all our contributors, for having the courage to share their fantastic work, and to Stephanie Jardine for the beautiful cover art and additional illustrations.

Thank you to all at Converge for all they've done to support this production.

And finally, thanks to our production team of Helen, William, Alice, Angela, Elaine, Gavin, Georgia and Sam for being the intrepid crew for this year's smooth voyage of the Great Ship Overly Ambitious!

About Our Authors

ANGELA BRIDGE is passionate about the written word in all its forms. She hasn't written anything for ages, but Converge writing exercises got her going again, so she's delighted to have put pen to paper again.

CAROL is a fitness freak, at the gym most days whether she wants to go or not, but it will keep her legs working! Now she's loving writing even though she never expected to!

CHAD COPLEY has been part of Converge for two years now and he writes about relationships with friends and family and his own experiences. He wrote the piece in this anthology because he was trying to understand something that had happened to him.

CATE WILDER is a pseudonym. Cate has utilised her writing in recent months as a means through which, she is able to promote the value of writing for social change. As a public health nurse, Cate has witnessed the impact of deprivation. She has witnessed the impact of suffering and she understands the real value of demonstrating compassion at a time when people need it the most. The importance of taking action when needed is what instinctively drives her. Having established her own Writing for Social Change group, she now inspires others to write alongside her.

CHRISTINA struggled to produce a piece for CWH7 and was about to give up. However, during a freewriting session, a picture prompt was put up of a person sitting on a bench looking out to sea. What drew Christina's attention was a small patch of rough wild grass, and sitting on the edge of the grass was a small, bright yellow flower. Upon closer inspection it turned out to be a dandelion which reminded her of her sisters and a game they played as children called tick-tock - but only once the flower had changed into a beautiful white puff ball.

This made her start to think along the lines of a wildflower story, with the repetitive sound in her head tick-tock, tick-tock. As she worked, it turned into something quite different - and that's the creative mind in creative writing.

DAWN SKELTON resides on the Northern English Coast, she is passionate writer, poet and artist. Creative expression has been a pivotal lifeline, aiding personal discovery and connection with a broader cultural community. In solidifying her role as a storyteller of experiences, she hopes to inspire others to embrace their voices and stories through creativity. Dawn has worked with Converge Connected and has published poetic narratives in CWH5, CWH6, and the final narrative of her trilogy here in CWH7. Dawn has deep gratitude for the educational opportunities offered by Converge, she thrives in public engagement with invaluable mentorship. Dawn continues to communicate through diverse multidimensional platforms. Dawn is currently working on her illustrated poetry book and autobiography towards publication.

ENOCH MCFADDEN has published work on the political economy of the body in post-industrial societies. He is a musician who writes detective fiction, songs, and social theory.

ESTHER CLARE GRIFFITHS is an author and songwriter. She loves to write with her dog snuggled up next to her – he's an enthusiastic audience and never quick to judge! She has published two compelling and poetic novels - Eliza Quinn Defies Her Destiny and Maeve Quinn Harbours A Dark Secret. They are available on Amazon in paperback and Kindle. She is currently working on her memoirs of growing up in a tiny cottage amongst the emerald hills of Northern Ireland, and an eccentric, terraced house in Durham – which was almost burnt to the ground when her Grandma came to stay!

HELEN KENWRIGHT is a writer, fangirl, gamer and musician who ran away to York from Croydon many decades ago. It was the best escape she ever made. She writes speculative fiction, romance and is currently working on a novel about secular cults. There are usually dragons.

JAMES WILSON is here for his third year on Creative Writing at Converge in York St John's university, and it has been a great help to him. In his spare time he likes reading, guitar and gaming. He has two nieces and a nephew.

JOHN F GOODFELLOW is a filmmaker, poet and writer; a proud member of the Writers Guild of Great Britain and a staunch advocate for inclusive education. He also paints, and takes photographs of York scenes. A true renaissance man.

JUNIOR CRYLE. The man. The Comic. The dragon-fanatic. Junior has been an active Converge student and frequent CWH contributor since Volume II. Whilst comedy is his main style, he is not afraid to experiment and learn with genres unfamiliar to him. All towards a goal to entertain everyone with his creative and imaginative works. Just don't remind him that poems don't have to rhyme, or that bread and butter pudding is a pudding. (He does not believe it.)

KAREN works for the Discovery Hub at Converge, supporting students to access and attend courses.

KEITH is from N. Yorkshire. He has done creative writing for a number of years. He is classed as a mature student, with a good sense of humour.

KEVIN KELD currently calls home the picturesque market town of Pocklington and shares this privilege with his invisible cat called Gerald. Author of the best-selling Motorcycle Undertaker detailing his forty-seven-year association with the humble two-wheeler he is now gathering together amusing anecdotes for a follow-up title. Interests and hobbies include comedy writing, Pink Floyd and robins. His ambition is to be placed inside a giant pork pie armed only with a fork and eat his way to freedom.

LAURAN is York born and bred. A big fan of horror and

true crime, she can sometimes veer off her usual path and end up down the rabbit hole. Sometimes she can even be funny. Lauran is mother to a black and white cat who likes to drink water from his paw, preferably from the tap in the bathroom.

L.D. ETHRAE was born in the suburbs of Aldvon on Covyn 5. She is currently one of the most prolific publishers on Ancient History for the Covyn Historical Society (CHS) and holds one of the chairs on their Board. Her best friend is renowned Project C, the only person in Covyn to publish more books on Ancient History than L.D. She currently resides in Lios where the headquarters of the CHS sits. L.D. spends her free time running around like a little girl hugging trees and chasing cats as well as going off to exotic archaeological expeditions with her friend Project C.

L.D.'s first book, *The Immortals of Covyn: Part 1* was published in 2021, and is available from Amazon. https://www.amazon.co.uk/dp/B09M6S8T1M

LORNA lives in a market town in North Yorkshire and shares her home with her grown-up offspring, a cat and a snake. When she's not trying to write stuff or keep up with her tap dancing, she is out on her bike or spending time with lovely friends. This is the first time her writing has been published and she's hoping it won't be the last.

MICHAEL FAIRCLOUGH is writing this at the last second and has to go to the shop to buy stuff. Also, he didn't put the bins out yesterday or the recycling and is annoyed about that. Currently he wants to make a snow globe and a pair of maracas and fill them with teeth he bought on Etsy. He released his first book, *Making Ends Meat* in April of 2023, available on Amazon: (https://amzn.eu/d/et8BElK). You can also find more of Michael's writing in the previous Creative Writing Heals books except for Vol 1, as the lollipop-people were holding Michael prisoner in Penryn at the time.

MINNIE lives in York with her husband and two dogs. She

is very creative and enjoys storytelling through acting as well as writing. She has been published previously in *Creative Writing Heals 4* and has had various pieces of poetry published throughout the years. She finds an unparalleled pleasure in stories because the imagination is a playground and anything is possible.

NIC CAMPBELL lives in Yorkshire with her very supportive husband (anyone else would run a mile) and her dog Alfie. She enjoys sewing and crafting, in particular altering clothes for her youngest daughter who needs them to fit for her performing arts job. For her eldest daughter, she keeps company on dog walks, coffee shops and non-stop chatter about hair and beauty. She has worked for many years creatively and passionately counselling Children and Young People in need of mental health support. She journals every day and would like to gather all her memoirs and make them into a book. In the meantime, she will find any excuse to try and get a swimming pool into her back garden (not a chance)!

PAUL FRANCISCO spent his childhood in Dorset before moving away for university. He studied at Winchester and has a First-Class degree in English with American Studies. He has worked in administration for the HE Sector and the NHS - as well as, more recently, for Converge. He has also sold ice creams. His hobbies have included making primitive home music recordings and, for several years, he was keyboardist in the Converge band 1 / 2 / 6. He dabbles in art but his current enthusiasm is performing his poetry on York's vibrant Open Mic poetry scene. He is currently putting together his first poetry collection. He has lived in York since 1998 and has been a Converge student since 2015.

SJL is fuelled by religious trauma, and still living under the cctv camera of gods all seeing eyes. With so many words in their head, they leak out of S J L at an alarming pace, Internal screaming from their brain converted to word vomit on a page for your viewing pleasure. Amen.

STEPHANIE JARDINE is an artist and illustrator who dreams of one day illustrating and publishing her own children's book. Her art is whimsical and often features fantasy creatures. When she's not creating she loves to play video games, such as The Legend of Zelda. She sells her art and crafts at York Fabrication, Etsy and the occasional stall. You can check her out on Instagram @stephsstuff_art and at Etsy: https://stephsstuffshopuk.etsy.com

SUE T is a busy mother of seven, with one grandchild. Coming to Converge is a release and gives her something for herself. She has found that Creative Writing is a way to express herself and is something she loves.

VIRGINIA still lives in York with her wife. She has no intention of moving; Virginia's three children still haven't become characters in a Miss Nicely story, but they should keep their eyes open as it will happen sooner or later. Virginia's first Miss Nicely stories were published in the last two CWH anthologies. Previously she had three poems published in Road Map an anthology from a Creative Writing class that she attended in Cumbria at the end of the 1990s; Miss Nicely will be taking a rest over the summer while Virginia spends some time on a new project, but there will be more Miss Nicely next year. Her motto is "Keep calm and carry on writing!"

About Converge

Converge is a partnership between York St John University and mental health service providers in the York region. It offers high quality educational opportunities to those who use NHS and non-statutory mental health services and who are 18 years and over.

Converge was established in 2008 from a simple idea: to offer good quality courses in a university setting to local people who use mental health services taught by students and staff. The development of Converge has progressively demonstrated the potential of offering educational opportunities to people who use mental health services, delivered by students and staff and held on a university campus. This has become the key principle which, today, remains at the heart of Converge. Born of a unique collaboration between the NHS and York St John University, Converge continues to deliver educational opportunities for people with mental health problems.

We offer work-based experience to university students involved in the programme. All classes are taught by undergraduate and postgraduate students, staff and, increasingly people who have lived experience of mental ill health. We have developed a solid track record of delivering quality courses. Careful support and mentoring underpin our work, thereby allowing students to experiment with their own ideas and creativity whilst gaining real world experience in the community. This undoubtedly enhances their employability in an increasingly competitive market.

As a leader in the field, Converge develops symbiotic projects and partnerships which are driven by innovation and best practice. The result is twofold: a rich and exciting educational opportunity for people with mental health problems alongside authentic and practical work experience for university students.

The aims of Converge are to:

- Work together as artists and students
- Build a community where we learn from each other
- Engage and enhance the university and wider community
- Provide a supportive and inclusive environment
- Respect others and value ourselves
- Above all, strive to be ordinary, extraordinary yet ourselves

About the Writing Tree

The Writing Tree is dedicated to the support and nurturing of creative writers. Founded in 2011, the Writing Tree offers tuition, e-format conversion and editing services and publishes work by community groups and other new writers.

The guiding principles of the Writing Tree are that creative writing has importance independent of subject, purpose or audience, and that everyone has the right to write - and to write what they wish.

The Writing Tree is honoured to publish 'Creative Writing Heals' for Converge. All profits from the book are donated to further the efforts of Converge writers.

You can find out more about the Writing Tree at www.writingtree.co.uk.